I0731511

A Warrior of Eden

G. S. Kenney

Copyright © 2022 by G. S. Kenney

All rights reserved. No part of this book may be reproduced, scanned, or transmitted in any form or by any means, electronic or mechanical, including photocopying, recording, or any information storage and retrieval system, without permission in writing from the author. Please do not participate in or encourage piracy of copyrighted materials in violation of the author's rights.

This is a work of fiction. Names, characters, places, and incidents are either the product of the author's imagination or are used fictitiously. Any resemblance to actual persons living or dead, businesses or organizations, events, or locales is entirely coincidental.

Cover art: JS Designs Cover Art, www.jsdesignscoverart.com

Praise for Freeing Eden

"From the very first sentence, *Freeing Eden* charms with compassionate characters, and seduces with its intriguing premise. If you're looking for adventure alongside your romance, this warm and beautiful novel delivers!"

– Elaine Isaak, author of *The Singer's Legacy* series

"An intriguing story, well told, set in a rich, unique world. Send in the clones."

– S. C. Mitchell, author of the award winning *Xi Force* series

"I read it in one sitting and then went back a week later and read it again, just to enjoy the detailed story and intense characters again."

– Amazon Reviewer

"A well-conceived journey of adventure and self-discovery."

– Amazon Reviewer

"...the planet Eden, is a cleverly conceived, intentional throwback civilization...Against this backdrop, the well-developed main characters ground the story in an intimate discovery -- of self and one another -- that keeps the reader engaged throughout."

– Amazon Reviewer

Praise for The Last Lord of Eden

"A deeply thoughtful, swashbuckling sci-fi adventure. You'll get swept away and lose track of time, as you race to the end, hoping beyond hope that Kell can save his home planet without betraying the woman he loves."

– Suzanne Tierney, award-winning author of *The Art of the Scandal* and *Blooms of War*

"Beautiful and thrilling, this book truly is the perfect Sci-Fi romance."

– NetGalley member review

"Skillful plotting and memorable characters abound in this well-conceived interplanetary adventure...So caught up in the fast-moving, intricate plot, I had difficulty leaving the book for meals or bedtime. Highly recommended."

– Amazon Reviewer

"Once I got into it I had trouble putting it down. (But you have to sleep sometime)"

– Goodreads Reviewer

Contents

Chapter 1

"Karoline." Arms crossed, Hendrik spoke sharply.

Karoline jumped, stabbing her finger with her sewing needle. "Ow!" She glared at her stepfather. He had just enough gray at his temples to impart the look, if not the substance, of wisdom. But Hendrik was always frowning, etching ever deeper those two vertical lines between his brows. And he was so bossy, nothing like her real father. Why had her mother married the man?

"What?"

"I want thee to run an errand for me." He used *thouspeak*, the way an adult addressed a child. As if he'd never noticed she was already fourteen, a woman grown. And besides, why couldn't he run his own errands, like everyone else?

She curbed her temper and held her tongue. "What errand?"

"I am going to hold a meeting of the resistance leaders. Go find Yosep and Katrina, and bring them to the meetinghouse."

Meadowcreek was not a large village. Like all the settlements on Eden, it was a farming community. Yosep had several fields of grains and vegetables he'd be out planting, and Katrina would be tending her large orchard, which had suffered some damage in last winter's storms. It could take the rest of the morning to find them. Why couldn't Hendrik wait until they returned home at lunchtime?

"I'm right in the middle of letting out the seam on this dress." *As he could clearly see.* "I'll be happy to go look for them as soon as I finish."

"Do it now," he said.

She held his gaze for just long enough to convey what she thought of his command, of him, and of her whole miserable life, forced to stay home like a child while the people around her went out doing important work for the resistance. She too wanted to play her part in driving the foreign invaders off Eden so that her people could live in peace. She wanted to be a Hero of the Resistance, like her father had been—not Hendrik's errand-girl. "I will do it," she said, "in five minutes, when I finish this seam."

Hendrik let out a dramatic sigh and turned on his heel. He walked out of the house, slamming the door behind him.

Karoline hated to think ill of a person, but Hendrik fell far short of what her father had been. Hendrik probably wasn't that bad, not really, not in the Great Scheme of Bad Things. Not like the creepy Black Lord, whose soldiers forced people to grow Andrea's daisy to make the evil addictive drug, and who killed people when they didn't obey. No, Hendrik wasn't evil like that, but he was never going to take the place of her father, even if he had come from who-knows-where shortly after her father died in a skirmish with the Black Lord's soldiers, then married her widowed mother, and wormed his way into the resistance leadership.

Even now, five years after her father's death, everyone still talked about him with awe. She heard it all the time: Yakob Keller, the Hero of the Resistance. Without him, her mother had said, they would all be forced to do the Black Lord's bidding, unable to live their lives according to their beliefs and customs, as their planetary charter had promised, and as their ancestors had once done in peace. He had united the people against the Black Lord and found imaginative ways to thwart the foreigner's plans. People called him Swifthammer, the greatest leader the resistance ever had.

No one ever talked about Hendrik that way.

Karoline tied the knot at the end of the seam, cut the thread, and took a moment to examine her work. The stitches were almost even. Someone with more patience might have made the seam prettier, more perfect, but this would be good and strong. It would do. She could let out the one remaining seam when she returned from Hendrik's errand.

Karoline hadn't minded that her father traveled near and far to lead the resistance. Mind? No, she was proud of him. What bothered her was that he'd never let her go with him. More than anything, she had wanted to fight by her father's side. He often used to took people with him, sometimes even her mother. But never Karoline. Never.

And then, just a week after her ninth birthday, he left, a painful departure like all the others, but this time he didn't return.

"He's dead," her mother had said. Marta had seen the Black Lord's soldiers shoot him with their projectile weapons. And Karoline learned a new word in the foreigners' language: guns.

Karoline turned the dress over to examine the outside of the seam she'd been letting out. It was surprisingly straight. The dress would last another few years if she didn't continue to grow too much. At fourteen, she already taller than her mother. Surely her growth years were behind her now. She packed her needle and thread into the sewing box, neatly folded the dress, and took them both to her room.

That was the problem with Hendrik. He treated her like a child he could order around, as if she were still nine years old, her growth forever frozen in his mind. *"Stay here, do this, don't do that."* She had complained to her mother about him, but Marta shrugged off her complaints. "Thou *art* still a child," Marta had said, addressing her by thouspeaking, just like Hendrik. She'd smiled, but at that moment

Karoline understood that neither her mother nor any of the resistance leaders was ever going to take her seriously. Not as long as Hendrik continued to demean her.

She was in an impossible situation. Karoline clenched her fists, letting the door slam as she left the house, and marched up the path toward Yosep's house. A stiff breeze raised goosebumps on her arm, and though the sun was not visible through the mist—as usual—the air was spangled with gold and copper glints that might have been reflected sunlight. Her father had told her that these mists and spangles and the illusions of changing distances were unique to Eden of all the settled planets. This was why the Black Lord's soldiers couldn't find their way around on their own. If the mist wasn't normal, Karoline wondered what other planets were like. Maybe one day she'd find out, but for now, this was the kind of perfect day on Eden that she liked the best. She began to relax as she walked.

When Yosep's house came into view, Karoline remembered something he had shared in Meeting last Sabbath, a thought that had struck her deeply. "It seems to me," he had said, "that often a problem one perceives in others can be solved within oneself." It was unusually insightful of Yosep, and now, as she walked, Karoline wondered if this might apply to her.

Maybe other people saw her as a child because she acted that way, asking, "May I do this?" and "Why won't you let me do that?" Maybe it was time to act like an adult and just do what she wanted. Adults didn't ask permission, or whine when they didn't get their way. Maybe if she started acting like an adult, she would be treated like one. She needed to participate in Eden's struggle against the evil Black Lord. She needed to convince the others to let her join them in the resistance.

But what?

After Karoline fetched Yosep and Katrina, the resistance leaders gathered in the meetinghouse. Six chairs were arranged in a circle in the center of the room, four of them already occupied by Hendrik, her mother, Uncle Arlen, and a stranger Karoline didn't know. As Yosep and Katrina took the two remaining chairs, Karoline quietly sat on a chair in the back, hoping they wouldn't notice her. And perhaps none of the rest of them would have, but Hendrik did. "Surely thou hast something better to do, Karoline?"

He'd thouspoken Karoline again. And this time, in front of all the others. Her face burned. "Fine," she said, her voice shaking. She stood and walked stiffly out the door, more determined than before to make them all see her differently.

Fortunately, the day was warm, and the meetinghouse windows were open. Karoline walked around to the downwind side, where she could hear their voices clearly, and she could carefully peek through the window, since Hendrik sat with his back toward her.

The sixth person present in the meeting was a waywalker from Owen's Spring, about five days' ride from here. He had raced his horse through the shifting mists and landmarks on Eden's surface to bring news to the resistance leaders in Meadowcreek. "There are soldiers at Owen's Spring," he said. He wiped sweat from his brow. "They have made it clear that we are to plant the daisy for them, or face, what they called it in their language, consequences."

Andrea's daisy, what all this fighting and killing was about. Growing this plant for the Black Lord went against the moral principles and simple, godly ways the Edenians tried to follow. It went against their *rights* as an independent planet.

"They have never come this close to Meadowcreek," Uncle Arlen said. "They must be a month's march or more from Castle Rock."

Katrina sat, shoulders hunched, wringing her hands. "Do you think they'll come here? They might, mightn't they? What did you say, it's only a five days' ride?"

"More like ten or twelve days for them," Marta said, touching Katrina's shoulder. "They can't move as fast as we do. But what do we do about it?"

"What *can* we do?" Yosep said. He looked around, as if the soldiers might even now be surrounding the meetinghouse.

Karoline ducked.

"They'll probably leave us alone as long as we promise to grow the damned plant for them." It was Hendrik's voice, and Karoline looked through the window again.

"Now, Hendrik," Marta said, "you're right that they'll go away now, but they'll certainly return in the fall for the harvest, and then what?"

"Well, we're certainly not going to grow the daisy for them, that's for sure." Uncle Arlen ran his fingers through his unkempt red hair. "I was against anyone lying to them last year, and I'm even more against it now."

"No, that didn't work out well last year," said Yosep.

Hendrik coughed into his elbow. Last year, he had suggested a deceptive strategy of feigned compliance, and the leaders had decided to give it a try. They had asked the nearby villages to *agree* to grow Andrea's daisy for the foreign warlord, but then *not* to actually grow it. It was a strategy that most of the villages, uncomfortable with the idea of growing the daisy, but even more so with the lie, declined to follow. And that had turned out well for those who refused to go along, but the Black Lord's troops had destroyed the two villages that had done as the leaders requested. Now Hendrik just shrugged. "I'm certainly open to other ideas. But whatever we do, we must do it quickly. It's already planting season again, and the soldiers have never ventured this close before."

"It's a quandary," Uncle Arlen said.

"They've already killed five people in Hendersonville and burned two houses," the waywalker said, "and who knows how many more before that."

"But we can't tell people to grow the plant," Yosep said.

Marta added, "They wouldn't do it anyway. It goes against all of our principles to be participating in the production of such an addictive drug."

Karoline shivered. She'd heard what the soldiers did to the villages they attacked: They burned fields, destroyed homes, and killed people. Was that going to happen here in Meadowcreek?

A silence fell on the group as they all considered the situation. At last, Hendrik spoke. "We have some time. Martin here"—he nodded toward the waywalker—"lives in Owen's Spring, and he knows the way well, so he got here quickly. The soldiers will have to find a waywalker, and since it's planting season, that alone may take a few days."

The waywalker cleared his throat. "I'm the best in Owen's Spring, that's why I'm the one who volunteered. And you can bet the Black Lord's men aren't going to go anywhere except maybe home again without a waywalker. So, yes, if they're coming this way, I'd guess you have maybe two weeks."

This was certainly true. Edenians learned as children to find their way in the woods by noticing and memorizing a series of waymarkers—more permanent features of the landscape such as rocks or uniquely crooked tree trunks and branches. Karoline herself was particularly good at it. But offworlders, confused by the way Eden's mists made the topography seem to shift and change, needed help to find their way along all but the most travel-worn paths. But Karoline didn't see how this fact changed things. If the soldiers were coming in two weeks or two days—they were still coming.

"That's why I think we have a real opportunity here," Hendrik continued. "We need more information, and I believe there's time to get it and still prepare appropriately. I'd like to return to Owen's Spring with Martin and investigate the situation personally."

What? This didn't make any sense. Why go off and "investigate"? Karoline's father hadn't done anything like that, though now that she thought about it, she did remember Hendrik had gone off by himself a few times before. Every time Hendrik had left, Karoline had a strong feeling that there was something furtive about it—something that he wasn't saying. Perhaps it was just that Hendrik seldom actually did things himself. He was always ordering others to do things for him, just like he'd made Karoline fetch Yosep and Katrina. He liked to be in control. So even if he did want more information, why would he leave his leadership position here in Meadowcreek and take a several-days' journey, rather than asking someone else to do it?

Karoline turned her attention back to the meeting.

After an hour of discussion, the leaders agreed to Hendrik's proposal. He would go to Owen's Spring with the waywalker. Like most Edenians, Hendrik would remember the path exactly, waymarker by waymarker, as he traveled it. He would not need a waywalker to return.

As she listened to the leaders form their plans, Karoline decided that she wanted to go with Hendrik. He wasn't her ideal choice of a traveling companion, but it sounded like the danger would be minimal. And if Hendrik was going to do some good for the resistance, maybe she could contribute in some way. Perhaps, with her fresh, unjaded viewpoint, she would spot something that was not obvious to Hendrik. Maybe a trip like this would make him realize she wasn't just a child anymore. On the other hand, if he was up to something sinister, then perhaps she could uncover it and show everyone that he wasn't the leader they all thought he was. She would prove once and for all that she was her father's true daughter, and not Hendrik's worthless stepchild.

Karoline approached Hendrik as he was packing. "I was thinking," she said. "I wonder if I might come with you."

He put down the jacket he was folding and stared at her. "Thou? Why?"

She clenched a fist but refused to let her annoyance get the better of her. She made her voice as reasonable as she could. "I might be able to help you, that's all. I know how to travel. My mother and father used to take me with them sometimes. Not when there was fighting, of course, but other times when it was less dangerous, like now."

Hendrik looked her up and down, his expression as full of distaste as if she'd been covered in mud. "I don't need thy help. Besides, the sooner I leave the better, and I'll not wait around for thee to get thy mother's permission."

Hendrik had an offworld bottle of some polished metal that looked like iron would if iron were trying hard to become silver. This "thermos," as he called it, could keep liquids warm for a day or more. It was an odd object, which he must have gotten from some trader before he'd joined the resistance and met her mother. He now filled it from the pot of stew that Marta had set to simmering on the stove. This would be his lunch, which he'd probably eat in the saddle. Dinner, Hendrik would get at the home of whatever family he and the waywalker stayed with.

Hendrik went out to the barn to saddle his horse, and Karoline trailed after him. He brushed some straw off the rangy gray animal.

Karoline refused to wheedle or argue with the man. She just wordlessly handed him his saddle blanket, then his saddle, determined to show him by deeds instead how useful she could be.

He settled his pack behind the saddle and took the bridle Karoline offered, nodding his thanks. He swung into the saddle. "Tell thy mother I should return by the Sabbath after next."

Karoline opened her mouth to make one last plea, but before she had a chance to utter a word, he gave the horse's flank a nudge with his boot and rode away.

Chapter 2

"Well, that didn't work," Karoline said to the empty path along which Hendrik had just departed to join the waywalker. Her fists were clenched. She grimaced and opened them wide, stretching the tendons in her palm. Hendrik made her so angry at times. She had to stop letting him get to her like that. She took a deep breath.

All right, then, it was time for an alternative plan. She decided to follow Hendrik. She would stay hidden and look for a chance to do something important for the resistance—something worthy of her father. Yes, if Hendrik wasn't going to let her travel with him, she would go anyway.

She decided to leave in about two hours, after lunch, and follow him on horseback, far enough behind that Hendrik wouldn't know he was being followed, but close enough that his trail would still be fresh.

After Hendrik departed with the waywalker, Karoline finished letting out the dress she'd been working on. She folded and packed it, and then followed Hendrik's example by packing a jacket as well. She put her pack under her bed, out of sight, then set the table for lunch. The stew simmering on the stove filled the kitchen with the aroma of onions and herbs, promising that the meal would be a good one. Karoline blew on a spoonful. It tasted as good as it smelled, but might use just a little more garden sage. She went outside and picked a few leaves from the herb garden, then chopped them and added them to the stew. She was just stirring them in when her mother Marta came home.

"Is Hendrik still here?" Marta asked.

"No, he left maybe half an hour ago." Karoline swallowed. She mustn't hesitate, or she'd lose her nerve. "I asked if I could go with him, but he said I had to ask you."

Marta put down the ladle and looked at Karoline. "You want to go with Hendrik? I thought you didn't like him."

Karoline put her fists on her hips. Hendrik was a long step down from her father, but she wasn't going to say that to her mother. They'd been through that discussion before, more than once. "What I don't like is how he constantly treats me like a child. But you know how much I want to travel and to help the resistance. I thought that if I went with him, I could show how useful I can be, and then he'd agree I could be more active in the resistance. And if he let me do that, then you and the others would too."

"And you asked him if you could go?"

Karoline raised her chin and straightened her posture. "Yes."

"And he said . . . ?"

"He said I had to ask your permission, but he wasn't going to wait for me."

Marta's lips tightened. "That sounds like a 'no' to me."

"But, Mama . . ." She smiled sweetly, in the way she knew her mother had trouble resisting. "You know I can catch up with him. It's easy."

Marta sighed and began spooning the stew into two bowls. "Yes, I believe you could. You were always good at playing those hiding and tracking games with the other children."

"I was the best. I'm as good as any adult, maybe better than most. He'll only be an hour or two ahead. Two people on horseback—they'll leave a clear trail, and I'll be able to catch up in no time."

Marta brought the bowls to the table, and they both sat silently for a moment, as was the custom, taking a moment to be grateful for the blessings they had been given. Karoline thought of her father and was glad for the years they'd had together and for the good he'd done for the resistance. Then she thought of Hendrik and was grateful that at least he seemed to genuinely love her mother. She tried hard, in this moment of grace, not to let her own feelings about Hendrik color her thankfulness.

"And if you don't catch up with him?" Marta asked.

"But I will. And anyway, even if I end up sleeping out in the woods tonight, it won't be bad." Her gaze fell on the old quilt from her bed, now rolled up as a spare blanket for the coldest weather. "I'll take that old quilt, just in case." Hendrik and the waywalker, of course, would be staying with families in villages along the way, enjoying the hospitality that Edenians offered to travelers. But Karoline couldn't do that because she had no intention of joining Hendrik. He'd just send her right home. Most of the villages were so small that if Hendrik stopped there for the evening, he would likely see her, or well-intentioned villagers would ask him about the young woman traveling alone just behind him. She couldn't risk having Hendrik find her, so she'd be spending her nights out in the cold woods. But no need to alarm her mother about that.

Marta reached across the table. "Look, dear, I know you're eager to be all grown up, and you really are, in so many ways. Why don't you wait just a couple of years? I'm sure all the resistance leaders, even Hendrik, will be more than happy for you to join them when you're, say, sixteen."

"Mama . . ." Karoline put as persuasive a whine into her voice as she could. "You and Papa were already working in the resistance when *you* were fourteen. All we're talking about is a few hours or so till I catch up with Hendrik."

"But what if you can't catch up with him before dark? Even the most experienced waywalkers can't find their way in the forest at night, even with a lantern. The mists are thicker there at night, and that makes everything look so different they can't rely on the waymarkers. You won't be able to see Hendrik's trail, much less follow it."

Karoline knew this was true, but she wasn't planning on catching up with Hendrik anyway. "I'll just camp out. You know I can do it. I've already been out with you and Papa when you were running errands for the resistance. Sometimes we slept in the woods, remember? And you showed me how to do everything. How to gather leaves and grasses to make a soft bed, what foods to forage for, and how to light a fire and safely put it out. I know how to camp out. This wouldn't be any different—and it's only in case I don't happen to catch up with Hendrik today, which is very unlikely."

Marta drew in a deep breath, then let it out. "Well . . . If Hendrik said it's all right . . ."

Yes, yes, yes. Please say yes. Karoline was afraid to say the words out loud. She silently ate her stew as her mother did likewise.

When they finished their meal, Marta stood and went to the stove. She stirred the pot. "You should bring some food," she said, "just in case you don't manage to join up with Hendrik before nightfall. I'll pack some of this stew for you into Hendrik's extra thermos."

Karoline jumped up and ran to her mother. She gave her a big hug. "Thank you, Mama. Oh, thank you!"

Of course, she wasn't going to join up with Hendrik. Not today, and not the next day, either. And that meant she shouldn't risk eating in the villages, at least not the small ones. After tonight, she'd have to forage. "If I do have to camp out tonight, this will be great for dinner. And this time of year, there will be plenty of food and water for Blaze, too. Also, I can forage breakfast. I know which of the forest plants are edible, and what's growing this time of year."

Marta nodded as she spooned stew into the thermos. "I know you do. Your father and I made sure of it." They had started teaching Karoline when she was just five or six years old, along with planting and reading and basic first aid. "You brought back some delicious cress the other day, and those pretty wild nasturtium flowers."

Karoline smiled. She knew she could travel on her own, but her mother's confidence in her was still reassuring.

Marta turned and handed Karoline the full thermos. "You know what to do if you meet some offworlder, right?"

"Oh, Mama, I can speak Trade just fine. You and Papa met with traders a lot, and you made me practice all the time."

"Yes, you're better at it than most of us—except those poor people who live near Castle Rock and have to deal with the Black Lord and his soldiers all the time. And what will you do if the offworlders you come across are soldiers?"

"But the soldiers are near Owen's Spring, right? So, if they're coming our way, maybe Hendrik will deal with them first."

Her mother got a faraway look in her eyes and smiled slightly, as if at a distant memory. "Hendrik is very brave and a good resistance leader, but he's not a fool. He won't face the soldiers single-handed, and neither should you."

What—did her mother think she wanted to get shot down like her father? "Of course not. I'll hide, and if I can't hide, I'll run as fast as I can."

Her mother nodded. "That's right."

"But if they're not soldiers, I'll be polite and helpful, as any Edenian would be."

"Good. I do believe you are prepared for this. You'll do fine out there, but try to catch up with Hendrik today. Hurry up and pack your things now. Do you want help?"

"No, Mama. It'll just take a moment, and then I'll saddle Blaze and be on my way."

Marta shook her head, smiling. "My very grown-up daughter," she said. "Where has the time gone?"

Karoline returned the smile. There was nothing an adult could do on this journey that she couldn't also do by herself. She would never be more ready. Even her mother had agreed. This was her chance to prove herself, and she was not going to let a little bit of potential discomfort spoil it.

After lunch, Marta went out to the orchard with Uncle Arlen to check the soil drainage, fertilize the trees, and trim any branches that might have been damaged in yesterday's storm. While they were gone, Karoline gathered her supplies, went to the barn, saddled her horse Blaze—a gentle, chestnut gelding that had been hers since he was foaled eight years ago—and set out in the direction she'd seen Hendrik go.

Her departure timing was perfect. Hendrik's and the waywalker's trail was still fresh and easy to follow. By tomorrow morning, though, their trails, as well as her own, would be cold, with grass and bushes restored by the nighttime humidity to their undisturbed states. Only the most experienced trackers would be able to follow any of their tracks then, certainly not anyone from Meadowcreek.

The biggest danger was that Karoline might travel faster than Hendrik and catch up to him. He hadn't said she couldn't join him, but Karoline knew that was what he'd meant when he said to ask her mother. So of course he'd express his annoyance and disappointment in his most condescending manner and send her back home.

It made her angry just to think of it. No way was she going to let that happen.

Five days later, in the early afternoon, Karoline approached a village she'd learned was called Sunnyside, a name she found ironic, since it had been raining all day. Sunnyside was located at a crossroads of some sort, the trail widening into a regular road on its outskirts. Karoline was proud of herself for managing well on her own, but until today the weather had been pleasant. Not today, though. Cold and wet and miserable, Karoline had decided to risk approaching the village, the first she'd entered on the whole trip, hoping for a quick bite to eat and a chance to dry off a little—she and Blaze, both.

She didn't plan to stay long; in this weather, Hendrik's and the waywalker's trail would be obliterated quickly. She hoped just to make sure she knew which way they left the village and then to stop on the outskirts for her own lunch.

The few people who were out ran, rode, or drove their wagons quickly, hunched over against the downpour, heads covered. Thank heavens the place was busy enough her own presence would not be particularly noted. Skirting the center of the large village, Karoline spotted two men standing in the rain in front of a house at the misty edge of visibility. As they talked, their voices drifted in and out with the mists, as elusive as shadows. The rain drummed out their words, but the way the one on the left stood, the way he gestured as he talked, and the intonation of his voice—it could only be Hendrik.

She dismounted and guided Blaze behind some trees.

As she watched, the other man clapped Hendrik on the shoulder, then walked toward the adjacent barn. He walked with one leg stiffer than the other—a distinctive gait that marked him as Hendrik's waywalker from Owen's Spring. A moment later, the waywalker came out again with his saddled horse. He mounted and departed.

Hendrik watched him go and then went into the house. Why would he be staying at the house, and not continuing on his way? And why had he dismissed the waywalker? Karoline could think of only one answer: This village must be Hendrik's destination. He had arrived—and that meant she had, too.

Karoline looked around. Sunnyside was more spread out than Meadowcreek; and Hendrik appeared to be staying in a large house near the center of it, next to the meetinghouse. She decided to find a place she might stay, down the same street toward the edge of the settlement, where Hendrik wouldn't stumble upon her, but she might notice if he left town.

As Karoline rode slowly down the street, looking for a likely place, a breeze brought the wonderful smell of something baking. Apple pie, almost certainly. Karoline inhaled the fragrance deeply, and it brought back a vivid memory of the last time she'd seen her father. He and his band of partisans had just returned from some splendid and daring act of defiance against the Black Lord and his soldiers, and she and her mother had baked apple pie for the celebration feast—apple pie that smelled just like this. Karoline smiled to herself. Neighbors brought dish after savory dish and breads and jams and desserts, but none of it could match the pies right out of the oven. The delicious fragrance came from a modest gray house. This was where Karoline wanted to stay.

At her knock, the door was opened by a middle-aged woman with a round face, gray hair, and a kindly smile. "Oh my," she said, "you are soaked to the bone, poor child, won't you come in and dry off a bit?"

Karoline had had plenty of time to prepare a story to explain her appearance alone, and she dove into it now. "I'm sorry to trouble you, but I—"

"Don't just stand there, come in, come in," said a man's voice from inside the house. In the dim light of the room, she could make out a man with curly gray hair, who was bent over the fireplace with a poker.

"Yes, do come inside," the woman repeated. "There's a fire in the hearth, you can warm up."

Karoline stepped inside. "Thank you. My name is Karoline. I'm on my way to Owen's Spring to visit my cousin. We grew up together, and now she's expecting her first child."

"Well, it's a terrible day for traveling. Can't your journey wait till the morning?" said the woman, still smiling. "I'm Lana, and this is my husband Gyor. We have six children. Two of them are still at home here with us. If you stay for lunch, you'll meet them. You will stay, won't you?" Without waiting for an answer, she continued, "The other four are grown and off on their own. So you see, we have plenty of room for you to stay the night, and perhaps the rain will clear by morning."

"Thank you," Karoline said, moving closer to the fire. "This feels wonderful."

"Lunch will be ready shortly," Lana said. "I cooked for only the four of us, but there's not much difference between four mouths and five. There's plenty for you, too."

What had been an adequate meal for their family of four was stretched to feed five, and it sufficed. After lunch, the rain let up. Her host family returned to planting a field not far outside of the village, and, claiming she needed a rest before continuing on her journey, Karoline resumed keeping watch on the house where Hendrik was staying.

The waywalker returned and joined Hendrik inside. He visited for only a few minutes—just delivering a message, perhaps, or arranging a later meeting—and then departed again.

Hendrik appeared no more that day.

Chapter 3

The next morning when the sky had barely begun to lighten, Karoline got up with the others in the household. After a brief breakfast, Gyor and Lana and their children set off to work in their fields, and when they were gone, Karoline again resumed her watch. An hour or so later, Hendrik emerged from the house where he'd been staying and headed out of the village on a small path Karoline had not noticed before. He carried no pack, and he went on foot.

Karoline checked the nearby barn and confirmed that Hendrik's horse, still unsaddled, remained within. Quickly, she returned to Lana and Gyor's to feed and water Blaze. Although she didn't know when she would return for him, she was confident that she would—for surely, Hendrik would not abandon his own horse.

On foot, Karoline found it easier to read the signs—the torn leaves and crushed undergrowth—where Hendrik had passed. She followed him for an hour, maybe longer. Just as she was about to emerge into a clearing, she saw Hendrik pacing back and forth. She drew back within the trees at the edge of the open area to watch, and to consider.

The clearing was obviously Hendrik's destination—but why? To Karoline's eye, it was just a field that had been harvested last autumn and not yet turned or plowed this season. It smelled of old hay and spring's fresh earth, with new wild seedlings already starting to grow in the rich earth. Perhaps the people of Sunnyside would grow that

Andrea's daisy here, the source of the evil drug the Black Lord wanted them to grow as a crop. She looked more closely at the weeds filling the furrows, seeing now that they were, in fact, mostly Andrea's daisy, growing wild as it did on Eden but nowhere else. There must be dozens, no, hundreds, of fields like this, all over Eden. People everywhere simply turned the evil weeds under and grew their crops. Such a field could hardly warrant a five days' ride to visit.

No, Hendrik must be planning to meet someone privately here, following specific instructions—instructions that, now that she thought about it, must have been delivered by the waywalker when he had returned to Sunnyside yesterday.

The edges of the clearing were lost in the thick mist, and the day was dark enough to suggest it might rain again. Even the occasional flashes in the air were somber and dark, like reflections off onyx, or coal, or steel. Hendrik stopped, adjusted his cloak, and straightened his collar. He peered all around into the heavy mist. At this distance, Karoline would barely be visible to him, as he was to her, but she instinctively shrank back behind a tree.

Hendrik took a breath and resumed his pacing.

Moments later, another man emerged at the far end of the clearing. He made no sound, and appeared suddenly, as if the mists of the planet had rejected him.

Hendrik reached the end of his pacing path, turned, and gasped. "I . . . You surprised me! I was beginning to think you might not come." Hendrik spoke not in Edenian, but in Trade. Until now, Karoline hadn't known that Hendrik spoke it.

The stranger made a noncommittal noise. He was tall and thin, a man of angles and bones, dressed all in black, even to the cap on his dark hair. He wore boots and a jacket, both of which looked new. On the shoulder of his jacket, some kind of insignia, too hazy to make out in detail, was embroidered in gold thread.

Could the man be from Castle Rock? Could he be—one of the Black Lord's soldiers? Karoline had heard that the Black Lord's soldiers wore black uniforms with insignia, but she'd never seen one of them. She looked carefully, but did not see a weapon except the knife at his belt, which was not very different from those that everyone wore. She had half imagined that soldiers were monsters, but, except for his above-average height, this man was definitely human.

"Did you." The stranger asked the question flatly, as if it were a statement. "I waited to make sure you were alone."

Karoline stayed behind her tree, grateful for the dark brown color of her dress.

"Of course," Hendrik said. "I'm pleased it's you in charge, Captain, and not someone I don't know."

So the man was a soldier, a captain, and Hendrik knew him. How could that be?

The soldier gave a curt nod but said nothing. Karoline became aware of the breeze rustling in the tree leaves.

"I need to know your plans," Hendrik continued. "If you and your troops are intending to march . . . in our direction, I will need time to prepare."

Karoline frowned. What an odd way to phrase his request. Why hadn't Hendrik simply asked the captain to lead his men back home? Or at least, not to march in their direction? What plans did he think the soldier had? And . . . time to prepare? For what?

The soldier made an expression that was almost certainly a smile, but stiff and a bit frightening. "Getting close to your home base, are we? Perhaps we could end this little resistance of yours here and now."

Karoline drew in a sharp breath. The captain's eyes flicked in her direction, and she stayed very still. After a moment, he turned his attention back to Hendrik.

"That would be a bad idea," Hendrik said. His voice sounded strained. "At least now you know where and who we are, and to some extent therefore you have . . . influence over us. But if you attack us, and we scatter or are destroyed, don't fool yourself. The resistance would continue, as it has for generations—but then once again you would not know who is leading it, whether one group or many, or where to find them. Or whether anyone might be willing to enter into . . . communication . . . with you again."

Karoline didn't quite follow everything in this speech, but "you have influence over us"? And "enter into communication with you"? It sounded to her almost like—she hated even to think it—Hendrik and the soldier were somehow working together.

The soldier sighed.

Hendrik pressed his point. "Your master would not be pleased."

"No, perhaps not. But he would also not be pleased if we return without obtaining the commitments we need, and as a result, the harvest is inadequate. Why don't you commit *your* village to growing the daisy, Hendrik?"

Hendrik's face turned pale. He took a step back. "If my people ever learn—"

The soldier gave Hendrik a look that might almost have been sympathetic. "We wouldn't want that, now, would we? My lord values your . . . friendship. Let me think about how to handle this. I don't know that we have gone far enough to ensure a good harvest. I'll review my notes tonight and make a decision; if we must go farther, I'll change the direction of our march and try to avoid your village."

Hendrik lowered his head. "That will do. Thank you."

Change the direction? But that would mean they'd just continue on to some other village, where people would be hurt or killed if they refused to grow that drug for the Black Lord. How was that going to "do," as Hendrik said? Karoline bit her lip. What kind of negotiation was this, anyway?

"I'll report this conversation to Lord Reuel when I return to Castle Rock. You will be safe enough from us—for now." He glanced up at the sky, perhaps trying to measure the time until evening. "Are we finished here?"

"Yes," Hendrik said, and then repeated, "Thank you, Captain."

The soldier turned, took four steps, and disappeared into the mist. Hendrik stood and watched him for a moment. Then he walked in the opposite direction, passing so close to Karoline that she could have reached out and touched him. But he seemed absorbed in his thoughts and walked by without seeing her, toward the place where he had stayed last night and thence, presumably, homeward.

Karoline hesitated. Should she confront Hendrik, or follow the stranger? But what could she accomplish with Hendrik? This encounter was puzzling enough that she wasn't even sure what questions she might ask him about it, and in any case he would probably refuse to answer. Worse, he'd be furious with her, and all that would come of her adventure would be his anger and her frustration and greater tension with her mother. How could she go back home again now? The mere thought of it was intolerable.

No, if she was going to confront Hendrik, she needed to know more. She would have to follow the captain, wherever that led.

The soldier hesitated as he walked among the trees, stopping frequently to peer at the bark of each of the larger trees. Karoline followed at what she hoped was a safe distance, barely keeping him in sight through the mists. When she passed the trees he'd stopped at, Karoline could see a notched-out mark he'd probably made with his knife when he first came this way. That, she thought, was clever. Offworlders, finding Eden's continual mists and shifting vistas confusing, never developed the knack of wayfinding, but this man had found a way to do something that had the same result. His marks were all identical, all at the same height, quite visible, and closely spaced. He would be slow, but as long as he was careful, he would return safely.

Return where?

Karoline fingered the notch that the soldier had cut into a tree and considered. Castle Rock was weeks of travel away from here. Was she following the man to a camp full of soldiers? That, she decided, was likely, and it was probably not a good idea.

"You! Girl! Hold it right there."

Karoline whirled. The soldier had turned back to face her. He held a weapon of some sort, and it was pointed toward her. It was too thick and chunky to be a knife; perhaps this was one of the projectile weapons the resistance leaders had talked about, the ones that killed her father. A "gun." Many of the soldiers carried them, but people said that on Eden the guns were not very reliable at any kind of distance.

In that case, it would be better to keep as much distance as possible from this man. Karoline turned and fled.

The soldier shouted, "Stop!" After a scant second, she heard his booted footsteps chasing her.

She ran into the forest as fast as she could, holding her skirt so that she wouldn't trip on it. Thank goodness she was wearing her gardening boots and not her Sabbath Meeting slippers. But even gardening boots were not made for running.

She could hear the soldier crashing through the forest behind her, and, with his long legs, he was getting closer.

She forced herself to run faster. Her breath came in gasps; she hadn't run this fast or this far since she was a child.

Behind her, the soldier was making a lot of noise as he ran through the undergrowth, but it did not sound like he was breathing hard. Soldiers, she knew, trained. They kept in shape. This one, for all she knew, probably ran for an hour every morning before breakfast.

And he was definitely getting closer.

The ground sloped downward, and the undergrowth was getting thicker. There might be water ahead; over the sound of her labored breathing, she thought she could hear a stream that . . . that she could cross and he couldn't? Not likely.

Ahead, between the trees, Karoline could make out a rock face. A boulder she could hide behind? Or a rock wall she'd be unable to climb? She'd have to take a chance. She ran toward it.

The man was close, she could almost feel his breath on the back of her neck. He would reach out any second now and—

Her foot caught in a tree root. She pulled it free, but she was off balance, falling forward. She raced to get her feet back under her body, but they just weren't fast enough.

She pitched forward, barely managing to put her arm out to protect her face.

It was so sudden that the soldier, already reaching out to grab her shoulder, catapulted over her, landing with a loud thud against the rock.

The wind had been knocked out of her, and Karoline gasped raggedly. When she could breathe more normally again, she tentatively tried moving her arms. The left elbow hurt, but nothing seemed to be broken. She sat up and looked at the soldier lying on the ground beside her. His cap had fallen off, revealing short, dark hair. He wasn't moving.

Her breath caught in her throat. What if he was dead? Worse—what if he wasn't?

Chapter 4

Maybe the best thing would be to leave as quickly as she could. Karoline slowly got to her feet. Her left hip hurt, and her right knee complained when she put her weight on it. But she was able to take a few steps. She would be sore, but she would heal. She took a few steps away from the soldier. She could get away from him, go back the way she came, and not have to deal with this injured and possibly hostile enemy.

No, maybe that was the *easiest* thing, but it wasn't the *best*. She turned back. The soldier still had not stirred. If he was injured, he would need help, and she was the only person there. It would be wrong in the eyes of God to turn away from a fellow human being who needed help. She'd never be able to live with herself.

Besides, this man had promised Hendrik he would keep the soldiers away from Meadowcreek. Perhaps he would even turn back to Castle Rock. It was important to keep him alive so that he could keep his promise. No, she couldn't just leave him there.

Her heart pounding, she moved closer and bent down. Her hand shook as she touched his shoulder. It was warm . . . but it would still be warm, of course. She followed his arm down, noting his torn sleeve, where a little blood trickled. It wasn't enough to have been fatal—a good sign. But then, he could have died from hitting his head too hard, with no bleeding at all.

She reached for his hand, and then searched for, and found, the pulse at his wrist. She let it beat against her fingertips for a moment, in sheer relief. Thank heavens, not dead.

Of course, this still left open the question of what to do about the man—the definitely-alive soldier who just a moment before had been chasing her with a gun. He must have hit his head when he fell, because he was still unconscious. He lay twisted over, and his right leg was . . . Karoline blinked, then looked more carefully. Yes, the calf had a slight bend in the middle, where the bone should be straight. Definitely broken. That was going to be painful when he woke up. Maybe more than just painful. There might be a serious underlying fracture. She needed to get him medical help.

The man himself was a problem, perhaps a serious one. If he died, no one would know he'd agreed to turn these soldiers aside, and his death would be on her conscience. But if he did awaken, might he still hurt her? He hadn't sounded the least bit friendly while he was chasing her, and there was that gun . . .

The gun, at least, was one thing she could take care of right now.

She looked around, and then spotted the thing, lying not far from his other hand. It was a dull black in color, and wicked looking. Her first impulse was to pick it up and put it in her pocket, to keep it from the soldier. But she didn't know what would make the weapon shoot its projectiles, and she didn't want to accidentally set it off. She studied it. There was a long part with a hole at one end. She didn't see any other place where the projectiles might come out. She also didn't see any place to put them in, so they must be stored in there somehow. A part of the weapon that stuck down from the long part was textured and shaped in a way that suggested this was where it was to be held.

She reached out with one finger and touched the part that might be a handle. The surface felt somehow hard and soft at the same time, and it definitely wasn't going to slide around in a person's hand. That left the notched part that looked to be made for a finger.

"Careful."

Karoline started, her hand jerking away from the weapon.

The man was looking at her. "The safety should be on, but it might have been released when I fell. Or you might release it by accident. Better yet, why don't you let me have that." He reached out.

Karoline stared at him. He'd know how to keep the weapon safe—but he'd also know how to use it on her. Giving it to him seemed like a bad idea.

His eyes narrowed slightly. "Do you speak Trade?"

"Y-yes. But I don't think I should give this to you. You might . . . want to harm me."

"And you might harm yourself—or me—by accident."

"Then tell me what to do."

"Just give it to me." He sounded exasperated and he was frowning. His face was lean and hard, with angular cheekbones and thin lips. There was grim determination in those dark eyes, emphasized by a pale scar that ran near his hairline from above his eyebrow to his ear.

Again, she felt the urge to run and involuntarily took a step away. But no, she couldn't leave him, not now when he needed her. Instead, she picked up the loathsome weapon by its textured handle and flung it as far as she could into the woods.

His shoulders slumped. "Now, why did you go and do that? How are we going to protect ourselves?"

"'We'?"

He was silent for a moment, as he tried to sit up. He let out a cry of pain. The lower leg was definitely not quite as straight as it should be.

"That leg doesn't look good," she said.

"Doesn't feel good, either." He reached down, but groaned and stopped. "Someone should probably take a closer look at it."

She thought about volunteering, but she didn't want to get near him. What she wanted more than ever was the exact opposite: to leave, and as quickly as possible. But how could she leave a person in pain, who needed help, even a soldier working for the Black Lord? She looked away, feeling his eyes still on her.

"It's probably broken," she said, breaking the growing silence. "You shouldn't walk on it. I . . . Maybe I could get someone from Sunnyside to look at it. A healer."

"We should do something about it sooner than that. If it's broken through the skin . . ."

Was he doubting her judgment, yet another adult treating her like a child? "If it is, what can you do about it?" she asked hotly. "Or . . . me. I don't . . ."

He pulled back, frowning. "Are you saying I shouldn't trust you? You wouldn't deliberately . . . hurt . . ."

She was horrified at the idea that one human being—that she—would further hurt someone already in such pain. "No! Certainly not. What kind of person do you think I am?"

"I think . . ." he said slowly, "that you are an Edenian, probably a partisan . . ." He gave her a long look, as if he was just now seeing her for the first time. The tenseness in his expression eased. "But no, you're probably too young to be a partisan, even for an Edenian. How old are you?"

She stiffened. Just like Hendrik, she thought. He thinks I'm too young to help. "Old enough to examine your leg. I've seen a broken leg before."

"Have you, now?"

"It was on a horse that didn't make a jump properly. The horse screamed too."

"Yeah, thanks. I guess we both know what happened to the horse."

"Well, it's different with people. If I come over and look at your leg, you're not going to try to grab hold of me or hurt me, are you?"

Something shifted again in his expression, perhaps a touch of sadness. "No. I won't."

She wondered if she could trust the word of a soldier working for the Black Lord, and gave him a skeptical look.

"On my honor," he added.

Karoline didn't know if she could trust his honor, either, but she realized that the soldier needed her alive more than he needed to harm her. She decided to take a chance. She approached him, knelt, and pushed up his pants leg. The leg was swollen, and it had an angle where no angle should be. "The bone is definitely broken." She didn't see any exposed bone, though. That was better than the horse.

"No kidding." He grimaced and wiped sweat from his forehead.

"It hasn't broken through the skin, though."

Once, when her father and mother and a band of comrades had returned from a campaign, one of the others had come back with a broken arm. Karoline tried to remember how it had been treated. She closed her eyes to bring the image back. Yes, the man's arm had been set, with two branches wrapped in strips of cloth holding the arm immobile. And they had tied the arm to his chest as well. "I don't think you should move it," she ventured.

"Can't. I'd probably pass out if I tried."

"Oh. It has to be made immobile, then, so you don't . . . pass out by accident. Or worse. If you move it the wrong way, you could make the break worse." She thought of how the horse had thrashed about before they put it down, the glistening white bone of its leg increasingly visible. She shivered. "Do you have any kind of bandages or . . . anything?"

"Not really. My men do, in camp, of course, but . . . Can you get back to the trail we were on? You Edenians can find your way around, right?"

"I was running so fast, I'm not really sure." She traced the waymarkers back in her mind. "Yes, I think I can."

"Good. Then listen, I want you to go back to the soldiers' camp for me. It wasn't far from where we left the trail. Ask for the medic; that's the soldier who has medical training. Bring him back—"

But Karoline was already shaking her head, horrified at the vision of being surrounded by enemy soldiers. "Oh no. I'm not going to the soldiers' camp. I'm pretty sure that wouldn't be a good idea."

"But I need—"

"I'll go to Sunnyside and bring back a healer." She folded her arms across her chest. "That will have to do." Could she get that done today? She'd walked an hour, almost two, from the village, no more than half an hour following this soldier, and probably another half an hour's walk to retrace the distance she'd run. Two hours of walking, no more than three, surely. Two or three hours there, some time to talk with people and find a healer, two or three hours back. No, there wasn't enough time left today before dark.

She thought back again to the man with the broken arm. How long had they waited before setting the bone? "I don't know if I can get there and back before dark, so maybe . . . Do you think we have to do something to set this bone before I go?"

He groaned. "Yeah, I think we do. That's probably true even if you just go to the camp. I had some medical training back when I was a grunt. Long time ago, but I'd know how to use the aluminum splints in the emergency kit." He paused. "If we had an emergency kit." He paused again. "Which we don't. Of course, there's one back in camp."

"Splints. Is that like sticks to hold the bone in place?"

He nodded.

She mimicked the unfamiliar word in Trade, then repeated it in Edenian to fix it in her memory. "We could use branches for that. And we can use fabric to hold them in place."

"That should work, but first we'll have to get the leg back into the right position." He gave her an assessing look. "I guess if we're going to do this together, we should be properly introduced. My name is Darrin."

"I'm Karoline. Pleased to meet you."

"So tell me, Karoline, are you squeamish? You think you'll be okay helping me to set a bone?"

She made a derisive noise. "I helped deliver a foal that was breach. This isn't any messier than that." At least, she didn't think it would be.

He smiled. It transformed the angularity of his features into something a little less intimidating. "Good. We'll make a fine team—the fearless helping the clueless. Shall we get started?"

"I'd like to get everything ready first," Karoline said.

He nodded. "Good idea."

"I'll start with the splints." She took the knife from her belt and walked around the area where they had fallen. "Why did you chase me?" she asked. "I wasn't doing anything to you."

"Why did you run?"

"Well . . . you're a soldier, aren't you?" She found a partly broken branch that might be good, about three centimeters in diameter at the break and fairly straight. It might not be strong enough for him to walk with, but it was probably sufficient to keep the leg in place until the healer arrived. And with a knife not made for sawing, she probably couldn't cut through anything much bigger. She broke the branch from the tree and began cutting two pieces from it, each a little shorter than his calf.

"And you're a girl," he said. "But I wasn't going to hurt you."

"How could I have known that? Besides, I'm not a girl."

He stared at her. "You're a boy?"

"I am certainly not a boy. I'm a woman."

The smile didn't quite mask his pain, but it seemed genuine. "My apologies. Of course you are."

"So tell me why you chased me."

"Because you were following me, and I wanted to know why. I wanted to know if there was anyone else with you, anyone I needed to be worried about." He made a show of looking around. "I guess there isn't, or they'd be here by now, what with the racket we made while we were running. Now it's your turn. Why were you following me?"

She began stripping the side branches and new leaf growth from the two pieces she'd cut. "I just . . ." What could she say? That she was spying on Hendrik and wanted more information? That would be the truth, but it might get her and Hendrik both killed. That she was hoping for an adventure—something bold and heroic? Either he'd laugh at her—or he'd assume she was a partisan and try to take her prisoner, and then she'd be forced to leave him, helpless here in the woods, to die. "I was just curious."

"About—?"

"I've never met a soldier before."

"Right." He gave the word a sarcastic lilt. "And it never occurred to you that approaching a soldier might be just a little bit dangerous?"

Karoline looked away from him, her gaze shifting right, left, right again. "Um. Well, maybe." She gave a small, nervous laugh. "But I didn't expect either of us would get hurt."

He reached out, palm forward gesturing her to stop. "Just a minute, young lady."

"Woman."

"Karoline. What were you doing out here in this meadow?"

There just wasn't any good answer. She drew a breath, looked him in the eye, and said, "Nothing you need to concern yourself about."

To her surprise, he laughed. "You were meeting some young beau, weren't you? Not one of my soldiers, I hope."

She was horrified. "No! Certainly not."

She finished cutting the branch and stripping the few leaves that grew from it, then examined her handiwork. The ends were rough, and there were uneven spots here and there, but the pieces were straight and solid. They would do, as long as he didn't try to put weight on the leg. "You wouldn't happen to have something to tie these with, would you?"

"Well . . ." Darrin glanced at her skirt, then away again. "At camp, we'd have rope, of course, or cable, but here . . ."

Karoline chewed at her lower lip, thinking. "Vines?"

"Maybe." He looked around. "But I don't see any. Do you?"

She'd been all around this spot when she was looking for a branch she could make into a splint. "No."

"How about my jacket? Cut some strips off the bottom."

She looked at the jacket. "If I'm gone overnight, you'll need this to keep warm. There's not a lot to spare."

"Overnight? I certainly hope you won't—"

"Just in case." She looked down at her skirt and looked around again. There was nothing else. All that work to let out the seams, and now . . . Well, she couldn't just leave the man. She sighed and took hold of the skirt's hem with one hand, her knife in the other. "Maybe I should cut a little extra, to protect your leg, so that the branches don't rub them too much. They're not exactly smooth."

"Thank you." He smiled. "But my pants leg will have to do. It's only for a few hours . . . or overnight, worst case. I don't want you appearing in that village looking like . . . well, not the way a proper woman should look."

Karoline considered. A dozen centimeters, more or less, off the bottom of her skirt would look a bit strange, but not terribly so. She started cutting.

When the materials were all assembled, Darrin took a deep breath and said, "I'm pretty sure we have to set the bone as straight as possible, so I'm thinking I can hold my leg at the knee, but you'll have to pull it at the ankle, and see if you can make it straight again."

Karoline nodded. "That makes sense, but it's really going to hurt."

He grimaced, jaw tight. "I know, but only for a moment. If we do this right, it will end up hurting me less."

She reached for his leg, then hesitated. Her chest was tight, and her hands had gone cold. She realized she'd never been this close to a strange man, certainly never touched one more than in passing. But this was necessary, and she'd already committed to it. She took hold of his booted ankle with both hands. "All right." And she pulled.

He let out a cry of pain. She gave a start and eased off.

"No!" He cried out a word she didn't know. "Pull it."

Karoline tried again, and this time, it didn't go as badly as she had feared. Darrin breathed a sigh of relief, and by the time she'd splinted his leg, he was breathing evenly, and color had returned to his skin. She settled him in as best she could and then set out to get help.

Chapter 5

It took Karoline longer than she hoped to reach the spot where she had started to run. Even in just the few hours she'd been helping Darrin, the planet's mists, ever shifting, had changed how the path looked. The day had grown darker, though the afternoon was probably no more than half done. Or had she lost track of time so completely while trying to deal with the captain's broken bone?

Karoline considered her options. She could see two, no, three notches up the trail toward the soldiers' camp; in the other direction, she could make out the next waymarker she'd noted coming from the village. If darkness fell while she was still on the trail to Sunnyside, she would not be able to see her waymarkers and would be stuck in the woods, alone and without any kind of food or shelter, until morning. On the other hand, Darrin had said that the soldiers' camp was not far. She might have enough time and light to make it to the camp.

But.

Despite herself, she shivered. Soldiers! The thought of being one girl alone—no, one *woman* alone—in a camp full of soldiers all night long . . . Darrin had promised his protection, but he would not be there to say anything to the soldiers. What if they didn't believe her? No, even with darkness falling, Karoline had only one real choice. She turned toward the village.

The mists shifted, making the air brighter as Karoline went; her time sense was not as far off as she'd feared. It was late afternoon when she reached Sunnyside.

She heard the commotion even before the village was in sight. Shouts broke the stillness of the forest air, sounding now distant, now close. Karoline was not sure whether she should hurry forward to help or run for her life. She compromised and cautiously crept toward the noise, moving from one hiding place to the next.

The village common was full of people. Perhaps a dozen soldiers brandishing weapons were forcing people to gather; a few soldiers led the inhabitants of the most distant houses. The soldiers shouted commands in Trade: "Line up!" and "You over there, get back in line!" and "Everyone in one group!" They emphasized their commands with gestures, and the villagers must have understood their intent, for they gathered as ordered. But they too spoke loudly, and in Edenian: "What is this?" and "What is going on?" and "We haven't done anything!"

"Quiet!" shouted one soldier. He was tall, and his voice carried over the others.

All the soldiers stiffened and instantly followed the order. The villagers' voices died down more slowly, likely because it took them longer to understand the foreign-language command.

The soldier lowered his voice to a more normal volume. "Someone here has kidnapped or murdered one of ours, and I intend to know who—or you will all suffer."

The villagers, apparently sensing the threat in the man's tone, huddled a bit closer to one another. A few people—those who knew some Trade—whispered to those around them.

The soldier made a disgruntled noise. In appearance, he might have blended in with the villagers, except for his uniform. But the noise was rude, and his manner was anything but Edenian. "Does anyone here speak Trade?" he asked in a tone that suggested he'd be surprised if they were capable of communication in any language whatsoever.

Whether because of fear or lack of fluency in the foreign language, no one answered.

"I will show you, then." The soldier nodded to a second soldier, a solidly built man who looked capable of lifting a wagon singlehandedly. "Sergeant, if you will."

The sergeant seized a child of about eight years.

The child screamed.

The sergeant held her close and put his knife to her throat.

Karoline's gasp joined those of the assembled villagers, and her hand went to her own throat. "No." Her mouth formed the word, but no sound came out.

The leader of the soldiers spoke very slowly and distinctly, as if his care in forming the words would cause the villagers to understand Trade. "Tell. Me. Where. Our captain. Is." He paused, then added, "Or. I. Will kill. This child."

The safest thing, Karoline told herself, would be to stay out of this. The soldiers didn't know she was there. She could leave. No one would expect her to help. She was just a girl.

But she couldn't leave. And she wasn't just a girl. That's what this whole journey was about.

Karoline stepped forward. "Wait." Her voice quavered, and she cleared her throat. "Wait. Threatening the child isn't going to help. Most of these people don't speak Trade. They don't know what you want."

"Savages," the man muttered. "So translate."

"There is no need." Karoline felt strangely calm, now that she had decided to reveal herself. "It's the captain you're looking for, right?"

The soldier glared at her. "Go on."

"Let this child go. Leave these people alone, and I will lead you to him."

The soldier stared at her for a moment. His eyes were pale blue, almost icy, and he wore an expression of distaste, as if he were looking at a slug. "Let the child go, Sergeant."

"Yes, sir, Lieutenant, sir." He released the girl.

"Take this one instead."

Karoline drew back. "Don't touch me!" She took a deep breath. "I know where your captain is, and I'll lead you to him. He can't walk. He has a broken leg."

"Right—or the partisans are holding him hostage, and they've sent you, an innocent-looking child, to lure us into a trap."

"What?" Karoline hardly knew where to begin unraveling this statement. "I am not a child. And no one is holding Darrin hostage."

The lieutenant studied her from tip to toe. He looked thoughtful. "But you don't deny being a partisan, I see."

"I—He has a broken leg. Otherwise, he'd be here himself, and I'd be gone."

The lieutenant continued to study her. "Your dress is torn. Either you've been in quite a scrap, or—"

Karoline drew herself up as tall as she could. "I do not. Scrap." She looked down at the roughly cut hem of her dress and the ungainly gardening boots revealed below. "I cut it to splint his broken leg."

"Right." There was an ironic tone in the lieutenant's voice. "And the sergeant here was just going to trim that child's hair. But, for argument's sake, let's say I believe you."

Karoline became aware of the knot in her stomach. She drew a deep breath. "Do you have a medic?"

"We're all trained in basic first aid."

"So is your captain. He needs more than just basic first aid. Let me ask if one of these people is a healer and can come with us. Perhaps then you can let the rest of them go back to their homes."

The lieutenant considered. "That means there would be two of you."

"Just me and a healer." She could hear her exasperation in her voice.

The lieutenant took his time looking her up and down. Then he smiled with no hint of warmth or good will. "Very well. I will have a squad of soldiers go with you. Eight soldiers should be more than sufficient to handle any little unpleasantness you and your partisan buddies have planned."

Karoline drew breath to respond in anger, but she thought better of it. Turning, she briefly explained the situation to the people of the village, ending by asking if anyone could set a broken leg. If a healer would come with her, the rest of the village could return home.

To Karoline's surprise, Lana, the woman she'd stayed with the previous night, came forward. "I will help you." She was heavyset with an ample bosom, a face that seemed permanently set in a kindly expression, and a twinkle in her eyes that reflected how much she liked everyone around her. "But unless this cap . . . uh, captain" —she spoke the new word awkwardly—"is very nearby, there won't be time to reach him today. We will have to wait until morning."

Karoline looked around. It was indeed getting dark again, this time with end-of-day finality. "I think he'll be all right over—"

"What did she say?" the lieutenant interrupted agitatedly.

"She's a healer. She'll help me, but it's too late to get there tonight. We can set out first thing in the morning."

The lieutenant looked around and grimaced. "Fine. Sergeant, escort these two ladies to our camp." Turning to the villagers, he made a shooing gesture with his hands as if they were a flock of chickens and said, "Go home if you don't want any more trouble. Now."

The people scattered. The soldiers clustered around Karoline and Lana.

"Wait," Karoline said. "Can't we stay here? You can come for us in the morning."

"Not a chance," said the lieutenant. "In the morning you'd be as gone as the captain." He squinted at her, as if looking hard enough would reveal some hidden truth. "And if we don't find him alive in the morning, you'll be as dead as him, too."

Karoline and Lana exchanged glances, but there was nothing to be done about it. Lana shrugged. "At least you won't be alone."

"Silence!" ordered the lieutenant.

This lieutenant was entirely too bossy—like Hendrik. Had Hendrik become bossy like that because he had once been in the army? But no, that thought was unfair to her stepfather. This man made Hendrik look positively kindly by comparison.

He made Darrin look good by comparison, too. True, the captain had been injured, but he'd been honest, maybe even a bit friendly. And Hendrik seemed to trust him. This man threatened children instead of simply finding a translator. He was . . . dangerous. Karoline shivered. She looked at the soldiers as they grouped around Lana and her. None of them looked at her. And none of them were smiling.

They entered the army camp shortly after dark. The soldiers set about feeding and grooming their horses, chatting in small groups, and getting their cook fires going. Two soldiers were assigned to triple up with others, and their tent was made available for the women. Inside, it smelled of sweat and old socks and who-knew-what-else, but it did give them some privacy. A meal of stew—overcooked from much reheating but still quite tasty—was brought.

Karoline thought of Darrin, alone and in pain. She wished the waymarkers weren't so hard to find in Eden's dark nighttime mists, so that they could return to him sooner. At least he would not be in danger, but by morning the poor man would be cold, thirsty, and hungry. She renewed her determination to help as soon as the morning was light enough.

Chapter 6

Soon the encampment grew quiet. Karoline and Lana settled onto the blankets they'd been given, but in the stale air of the closed tent, sleep did not come easily. Karoline tossed and turned for what seemed like hours.

A sound startled her, the gruff voice of a soldier who was obviously trying to whisper, muffled by the fabric of the tent. "Hsst. Ladies."

Karoline grabbed Lana's arm. It was still dark, what could the soldiers want with them?

Lana put her hand over Karoline's, clutching it tightly. "What is it?" she whispered in Edenian.

"Ladies, please."

Somehow Karoline found the voice to answer. "What?"

"We have to talk," the soldier said.

Karoline looked at Lana but could barely make out her face in the dark tent. She translated the request. "I think we should hear what he has to say."

Lana nodded, giving Karoline's hand a gentle squeeze.

"All right," Karoline said to the soldier.

"Inside the tent. Quietly."

Karoline translated for Lana, who shook her head slowly, seeming to express doubt that the soldier was up to anything good.

Karoline considered. Her own heart was pounding. What could they do if one or more armed men came inside their tent, in the dark? Then again, the soldier could have barged right in, no need to pretend he just wanted to talk. She said, "I think we have to take the chance."

Lana shrugged, then wrapped her blanket around her shoulders.

"Come on in, then," Karoline said to the soldier in Trade, "but leave your weapons outside." She lit the lantern inside the tent.

There was a shuffling noise, probably a weapon belt being removed, and then the tent flap opened. Hunched over to get through the low entry, the soldier came in. He held out his hands to show that they were empty. "No harm," he said, then added, "You are safe. One of my men is standing guard outside."

Safe from what? The other soldiers? Karoline felt her stomach tighten, but she said, "Sit down"—she tilted her heard to indicate a spot near the entry, as far as possible from where she and Lana sat—"and tell us what this is about."

The soldier groaned as he lowered himself to the floor. "Old joints," he muttered. And indeed, the man was older than most of the other soldiers, with close-cropped gray hair and wrinkles on his forehead and around his eyes. "Name's Ken. I'm a corporal, been with this army for twenty years," he said. "Got a good squad of men, and I like it here well enough. There's not much fighting compared to some gigs you can get, the pay is good, and this Black Lord here now, well, he's always been fair." He spoke Trade with a thick accent—from some planet she'd never heard of, no doubt—but Karoline could understand him well enough.

She translated for Lana. The man's perspective was interesting, but she wondered when he was going to tell them why he was there.

"I don't hold much with the officers, now," the soldier continued, "not that they ain't that bad everywhere, but the Captain here, he's the best of the bunch. Best commanding officer I ever had." He tilted his head and looked from Karoline to Lana, then back again.

Clearly the man was looking for some kind of reaction from her, but Karoline didn't know what. She tried a noncommittal "That's nice."

"It's more than nice." He'd raised his voice, and Karoline put a finger to her mouth to remind him to keep his voice low. He obliged. "Listen, when I was newly made a corporal with a squad of my own, we was out on patrol one day, and we ran into an ambush. We was in a steep kind of a valley, see, and suddenly these rocks came rolling down all around us from both sides. Well, we split and ran every which way, and when the rocks stopped rolling, we tried to form up again. But one of my men was missing. Probably dead, of course, but could have just been injured or unconscious or something. I called and called for him, but—nothing.

"The sergeant, he says we got to go, don't want to give them partisans time to set up another rock shower, you see? But I felt responsible for my men and didn't want to leave the one, especially since we didn't know whether he might be alive. There's only so far you can push arguing with your commanding officer without it being insubordination, but you better believe I pushed it. I begged for more time—an hour or two to run a patrol all around, but he says no." He drew a breath and looked off into the distance.

Karoline didn't know where this was going, but it wasn't much different than listening to someone rambling on in Meeting. Sometimes a person just needed time to circle around before they got to the heart of the matter. "Go on."

"Yes'm," Ken said. "So while we was arguing, the captain comes up—he was just a lieutenant back then, and the commanding officer of that operation. He asks the sergeant what the problem was, and he told him, and the captain says, 'Smart order, Sergeant, get your other two platoons ready to leave now. I'll keep an eye on this one.' That way, you see, the sergeant felt good and didn't have to bring me up on a charge of insubordination, but meanwhile, I got time to look for my missing man."

Karoline's curiosity got the better of her. "And did you find him?"

"Yes'm, I did. He'd been knocked out by one of them rocks, which is why he didn't answer when we called, and got trapped under a tree branch that came down. But we was able to free him okay, and other than that he wasn't hurt, and he's okay now. Saved his life, the captain did. Like I said, a good officer." The corporal took a deep, appreciative breath and let it out slowly. "So now, my man standing guard outside right now, name of Orton, he has something he wants to tell you, if you don't mind inviting him in."

That would be two soldiers inside their tent, but Karoline no longer felt that Ken and his man would be any danger. She checked with Lana, and the two women agreed.

Orton had a long, gangly frame, and he settled awkwardly into a sitting position, cross-legged on the tent floor. "Hi," he said. He was blushing.

Karoline smiled. "Hello, Orton. Ken says there's something you want to tell us."

"Yes'm." Orton looked at his commanding officer, who nodded. "Well, I guess the corporal here told you how I was rescued that time we were ambushed."

"Oh! He didn't say it was you."

"Yes'm, it was. Well, anyway, I was assigned to wait on the lieutenant this evening while he was eating."

Army procedures were a mystery to Karoline, so she glanced over at Ken. He nodded. "Standard procedure. Different squads take turns. The lieutenant likes to use Orton because they're all Kestran, him and the ones he's closest to. Most of us are, actually, but Orton here is from Brancnova."

Karoline looked at him blankly.

"Brancnovans don't speak Kestran."

"Oh. So they could be waited on and still have a private conversation."

"Yes'm," Orton continued. "Only thing is, my mother was Kestran, so in fact I do know the language. I don't speak it because I never learned the men's dialect, only the women's. The first—and only—time I tried speaking Kestran after I enlisted, they almost laughed me out of boot camp, teased me for weeks afterward. So I don't speak it no more. But I can understand it well enough."

"I see. And tonight you overheard something the lieutenant and his men said in Kestran."

"Yes. Right." He swallowed. "Yes. They're aiming to kill the captain and blame it on you. And then they're going to kill you, too."

"What?" Karoline looked from one soldier to the other, and they both stared somberly back at her. "Why? Why would they want to kill their own captain?" Not to mention herself and Lana.

"Lieutenant's looking for a promotion, see? Empty captain position opens up . . ."

Karoline shook her head, disbelieving. "He'd *kill* him for that?"

"Good jump in pay, plus all kinds of other opportunities." The corporal rubbed his thumb and forefinger together. "*Good* opportunities."

"But then why blame it on me? I'm just . . ." She almost said, "a child," but thought better of it. "I'm just trying to help."

"The help the lieutenant wants ain't the kind of help the captain needs," Ken said. "Lieutenant wants a scapegoat, but the captain—he needs help so he don't get murdered. That's why we're coming to you, see? We know you're trying to help the captain, and we want to help, too. The captain, why, he's done us both a good turn—"

"Saved my life," added Orton, "and now I want to help save his."

"So you got to go," said the other. "And right now, before it gets to be daylight and everyone's up. Get as far away from here as you can."

"If the lieutenant don't got nobody to blame, then he can't kill him, right? So hurry, get your things."

Karoline started to get to her feet, then paused. "No, wait. I'm the only one who knows where your captain is. If I don't bring him some help, then he still could die—from exposure, from hunger. Maybe from infection if his leg doesn't get treated properly. I can't leave because you can't find the captain without me."

Ken stared at her with a hard gaze, and Karoline again felt a knot in the pit of her stomach. She wouldn't like to be on his bad side. "You can't help him if you're dead. After you get away, you and this lady"—he nodded toward Lana—"can go find the captain. Get him somewhere safe."

Karoline's frustration was growing. "How?"

Lana and the two soldiers all put their index fingers on their mouths, and Karoline realized she had almost shouted. She lowered her voice. "He can't walk on that leg. Can't one of you come with us to help?"

Both soldiers shook their heads. "That would be desertion," Ken said.

"The punishment is death," Orton added. "We'll help from here as much as we can, but you got to get out of here and go help him by yourselves."

Karoline was already beginning to figure out what they would have to do. "All right. We'll go, but we'll need good medical supplies. Bandages, splints, and—what's the word in Trade?—disinfectant. Can you get them for us?"

Ken nodded. "We'll get them." He gave Orton a sharp nod. "Private Orton."

"Yes, sir," Orton said, and slipped out of the tent.

"Ken, if it doesn't put you and Orton in trouble, you might also tell anyone you trust who will listen, that we went to help Darrin. They have to know that we didn't just run away."

Chapter 7

With a pack of medical supplies from the camp and the two soldiers as guides, Karoline and Lana slipped away from the camp and into the woods. When the lights from the campfires began winking out of sight in the mist, the soldiers wished the women good luck and headed back to the camp.

Karoline had never tried traveling at night, but now she could see why her mother said it was impossible. In daylight, directions seemed to shift and distances to alter, but tonight the mists hung so thick and dark she doubted even a lantern would help. She'd be lucky even to find the next waymarker, never mind following from one to the next. Karoline and Lana retreated a few steps from the path and settled in to wait for daylight.

The mist had barely begun to lighten when Karoline was awakened by shouting and commotion from the nearby army camp. She touched Lana gently on the arm, then put a finger to her lips. The two moved as quietly as they could farther back into the woods and waited.

A moment later, a squad of soldiers rode by briskly, heading toward Sunnyside.

"My family!" Lana whispered, her face a picture of anguish. She took a step toward the road.

Karoline took a firm hold on her arm and pulled her back. "The only thing you and I can do for them is to get the captain back as quickly as we can. If Ken and Orton did their job, even that lieutenant will have to give us some time before he takes any kind of revenge on the villagers, don't you think?"

Hand to her chest, Lana took two deep breaths. Then she nodded. "Yes, all right. Let's go."

Cautiously, they went back to the road. The day had grown light, but without the flashes and sparkles that enlivened most days. Instead, the nighttime darkness seemed to linger here and there, shadows shifting without any light source, parts of the landscape disappearing as if they had never existed, only to reappear in some surprising direction a moment later. Listening carefully for the sound of soldiers coming or going, Karoline used the notches that Darrin had carved into the trees as her waymarkers, until she came to the one where the previous day she had left the road with Darrin chasing her. It seemed so long ago.

Karoline continued to read waymarkers as she retraced her path into the woods, while Lana walked behind her. "I shouldn't have volunteered to help you," Lana said glumly, her voice a dull monotone.

"I'm sorry." Karoline really was sorry. She couldn't stop imagining the soldiers doing terrible things to Lana's two children, to her caring husband. "But you are a healer. You did the right thing before God. We must believe that we'll get out of this all right, and your family will, too." She certainly hoped they would.

"Do *you* believe that?" Lana asked.

Did she? "I believe that we must act in the best way we can, or how can we live with ourselves? We owe it to our families and ourselves to be the best human beings we can be. And for us, right now, that means we have to bring the captain back before dark."

She realized she'd missed a waymarker while they were talking, doubled back to the previous one, and headed in the correct direction.

"If we can even get there before dark," Lana muttered.

"Of course we will. It's not that far. And while we're walking, let's go over how this is going to work. I have a plan, and I hope you can help make it even better."

As they talked, the air cleared and brightened. Less than an hour later they arrived. The mists were now a mellow gold that made the place look like a picture out of a storybook, except for the man lying near the rock, his leg swathed in bandages made from the fabric torn from Karoline's dress.

Darrin must have heard them approaching, for he sat upright, his features set in a fearsome frown, his knife in his hand ready to throw.

Lana let out a squeal and pulled Karoline toward her.

Karoline's heart thumped wildly, but no, they were there to help Darrin. Surely he wouldn't want to harm them.

"Oh, Karoline, it's you." Darrin sheathed his knife. "I'm sorry, I didn't mean to frighten you." He nodded toward Lana. "Either of you. I just didn't know who might be coming, or . . . why. It's been a long night."

"This is Lana," Karoline said. "She's a healer from Sunnyside."

"Hello, Lana, nice to meet you."

Recognizing her own name, Lana nodded a greeting to the soldier, but then she looked at Karoline, her eyebrows raised in a question.

Karoline said to Darrin, "She doesn't know Trade, but I'll translate." When she did so, Lana nodded again, then said, "May I look at your leg?"

Karoline again translated, and Darrin said, "I'd be most grateful."

Lana knelt beside the injured the captain to examine his leg. "This is very well done," she said.

Karoline's heart lifted with pride at this praise. She smiled. "Thank you."

"Do you have training as a healer?"

"Not really, no. We kind of figured it out together."

"Then perhaps you could become a healer, or you—or both." Lana nodded to Darrin.

When Karoline translated, Darrin shook his head slowly, but with a glint of humor in his eyes. "I already have a vocation, thank you, and it suits me just fine."

"Ah. You don't wish to change professions?" Lana continued. "That's a pity. More healers are what we need here on Eden, not more soldiers. But never mind. Your soldiers have given us better supplies, so I will bind the leg up again." She unwrapped the makeshift bandages. Then she frowned at the branches that had been used as splints.

When she touched Darrin's leg, the captain winced but did not cry out. Karoline instinctively reached out toward him, then suddenly shocked at her own forwardness, she drew her hand back.

"The leg is swollen," Lana said. "And bruised. When you return to the camp, check for internal bleeding. Inside the leg, you understand?"

Again, Karoline translated, and Darrin nodded.

"Now, tell me," Lana continued, "can you feel your toes?"

She touched Darrin's toes, which twitched. "If you tickle me," Darrin said in an exaggeratedly serious tone, "it will be my soldierly duty to kill you."

Upon hearing the translation, Lana blanched.

"He's joking," Karoline said.

Lana nodded. "That will be a yes, then. Good. But when you get back, check the feeling in your toes again, understand? You don't want to lose nerve function. Now let's take a look at the splints the soldiers gave us." She unwrapped the medical package, revealing a set of metal frames backed in some soft material, a metal can of something, tubes of ointment, and bright white bandages.

"These fit around my leg after you re-bandage it," Darrin said, indicating the metal frames, "but first you spray this on the inside." He pointed to the can. "It will become a dense foam, and when it gets firm, it will fit the splint exactly to my leg and provide some support. Then the rest of the bandages go around the whole thing to hold it tight. I did this in basic training a long time ago. Never thought I'd have to use it on myself one day."

Lana cut away Darrin's pants leg and wrapped the bandage around the leg. "These are very impressive," she said, examining the metal splints. "Now I'm going to use them to tie your leg up again."

"Um, Darrin... meanwhile, there's something you ought to know." Karoline said as Lana worked on the leg. "I believe a lieutenant of yours means you harm."

"What? That's hardly likely, but tell me what makes you think so."

She told him everything that had happened after she left, finishing with what Ken and Orton had said the previous night.

The angles of Darrin's face seemed to grow more pronounced as he clenched his jaw and tightened his lips. "I believe *you*—but I'm not sure I believe your informants. I've worked with Lieutenant Valdar for a year now, and he's a good soldier and an able leader."

"Do you think they were lying?" Karoline said, her voice raised angrily on their behalf. She took a breath to calm herself. "Why would they? They took some risks just to warn us and to get these medical supplies. They were trying to save your life."

Darrin winced as Lana tightened the remaining bandage to hold the splints in place. "I don't know what to think," he said. "If your two informants had come with you, I could question them, but obviously—"

"They didn't want to get killed for deserting."

He replied in a measured tone. "They would not have been deserting if they'd brought you to me. The proof of their intentions would have been in their actions. At worst, it would have been disobeying orders." He paused, looking away. "But then again, they probably also did not want to have to testify against their commanding officer. All the more so if they're lying. It will be hard for me to dig down to the truth of this when I get back, but I will do it, I promise you."

"*If* you get back," Karoline said. The lieutenant had threatened to kill an innocent child, while Ken and Orton had talked of saving lives. Maybe Darrin didn't know who to believe, but she had no doubts. "If that good-soldier lieutenant of yours doesn't kill both of us first."

"What—kill you? Why would he? You wouldn't be going to Castle Rock to tell Lord Reuel what happened, now, would you?"

The very idea filled her with terror. "Certainly not. But I might be telling a lot of soldiers what I witnessed, and some of *them* might be going to Castle Rock. He wouldn't chance it."

Darrin said nothing. Karoline hoped he was at least considering what she'd said. She sighed. This whole ordeal had been exhausting. She had no energy to even think about what lay immediately ahead.

She picked up the discarded old bandages—the fabric she had cut from the bottom of her skirt. She considered how she must have looked to the soldiers and the villagers both, with her hem all ragged and too short, showing the tops of her gardening boots and part of her bare calves. Had she been too bold? She tried matching the cut fabric to the bottom of her skirt, but the cut was too rough. Still, Karoline thought, she could sew a piece in a contrasting color along the hem, or perhaps as a band between the two parts of her skirt. It would be pretty. A little fancy, perhaps, but some midnight blue with the dark brown of the dress would be striking. Or maybe even a deep, dark red.

She smiled, imagining that Hendrik would be upset at such daring. Yes, she would hem the skirt with red.

Hendrik! Karoline gasped out loud, and Darrin turned to look at her. Hendrik would probably be getting home in a couple of days, and—if she survived Valdar's plans, however that played out—she would be arriving home a day or two behind Hendrik. He'd be concerned about her, and her mother would be frantic.

"There." Lana finished taping the bandage and got to her feet. "That's as good as I can make it. This cast seems very strong. You might be able to stand now, but still, do not put any more weight on that leg than you have to." Karoline continued to translate.

"Thank you," Darrin said. "You've been very kind."

Lana smiled and gave him a nod. Then she looked away. "Tell him, Karoline, if you don't mind, I must go to my family. My children are still young; they should not have to face this danger without their mother."

"What danger?" Darrin asked when Karoline translated. "Surely, the soldiers wouldn't—"

"They've already threatened. They believe your injury is a trick of the resistance, and they mean to make the people of Sunnyside pay."

Karoline translated, then said, "I don't think they'll do anything right away. They'll wait a few hours to see if they can learn a little more about what has happened to you."

"Then I promise you, Lana, if it is within my power, I will not allow any harm to come to your family. And if your family has been treated roughly, any soldiers who did so will be punished."

After hearing the translation, Lana said, "Thank you. It's difficult with the soldiers this close to the village. We are a peaceful people, but it's too easy for them—for you—to blame us for anything that goes wrong."

"We will leave this area tomorrow. You have my word. But Lana—we'll be back at harvest time. Why don't you see if you and your neighbors can grow some of that Andrea's daisy this year, okay?"

The villager looked away. "We are not in favor—"

"I know. And I know that your planetary charter gives you the right of self-determination. But there are politics—politics at the highest government level, far beyond you and me and even all of Eden—that come into play here. And if we can't get some of the daisy from you when we come back in the fall . . . I appreciate how you've helped me, and I don't want to be in the position to do you and your village harm, not now, not in the fall, not anytime. Do you understand? Even a token amount would be sufficient. Even a small token."

It was as long a speech as Karoline had ever heard the captain make, and she translated it carefully. She thought he was being honest, even though she still did not understand all his reasons. She remembered the arrangement Darrin had made with Hendrik, too. The captain seemed like a reasonable person, not ill-disposed toward her people. She began to see that Hendrik's relationship with the man—however it might have come about—might possibly be a good thing for the Edenians.

Lana said nothing.

"Perhaps we could pay you for the . . . trouble?" Darrin said. "How about some medical supplies? Bandages, antiseptic, maybe half a dozen splints or so? Lana, please. Let's make this work."

Karoline gripped Lana's arm before the older woman could answer. "I know a field near Sunnyside where the daisies are growing wild. I'll show you the one I mean, if—no, *after* this is all over. Just leave that field fallow this year, and there'll be plenty of daisies. All you'd have to do when harvest time comes around is just show them where it is."

Lana nodded, considering. Then she said to Darrin, "The medical supplies would be welcome. I'll see what I can do. No promises, but—maybe something. Even, as you say, if it's just a token amount." She smiled at him.

Suddenly, Karoline had another idea. "While we're making a bargain here, there's something I want, too."

Darrin arched a questioning eyebrow. "Go ahead."

"I want you and your soldiers to turn back. Your men have threatened this innocent village. By now, they may have even killed someone. You have your agreement"—she nodded toward Lana—"just as you wanted. Go home before something even worse happens."

"I assure you, we need the commitment of more than one village."

She met his gaze and held it. "I'm sure you already have it, all the distance you've come. I am asking you as a favor—decide that you've come far enough, and go back to Castle Rock."

Darrin studied Karoline for a long time, and she held his gaze. "This is far enough," she repeated. "I am *asking* you."

He spoke slowly, as if he were preparing a difficult argument. "Probably . . . I should report this incident to Lord Reuel . . . the sooner, the better. And I do have . . . a great many commitments . . . maybe enough." He nodded, as if the debate with himself had just been decided. "Yes, I believe I should bring the men back home now."

She could almost have sworn he winked at her.

"You make a convincing argument, Karoline," he continued, "but now it's my turn to ask a favor. This one is for your own protection. If you wouldn't mind, could you please help me find my gun? Then you could leave together with Lana. You'll be safe, and I'll take my chances with Valdar."

"No," Karoline said.

"I won't shoot you."

Was there a slight smile on his face? Karoline wasn't sure.

"I didn't mean, 'No, I won't help find your gun.' I meant, 'No, I'm not going to leave you.' I didn't go to all this trouble to help you only to have that man come along and shoot you, and blame me for it."

Darrin looked at her in a squinty way that seemed to suggest she wasn't making any sense. "And how is your staying here going to prevent that?"

Karoline drew a deep breath. The air smelled fresh and clean, as if the planet's mist carried extra moisture today. And perhaps it did. Perhaps it would rain. She let the breath out. "Because Lana is going to go home and make sure her family is okay. It'll take her maybe two or three hours, so meanwhile you and I will begin walking out of here together. I'll help you as best I can. And then she is going to come back with a wagon if possible, or at least with a larger, stronger person you can lean on, along with plenty of witnesses. Once you're back among your soldiers, then I think you'll be safe."

"Thank you for looking out for me, Karoline." There was amusement in his voice, just the way her father sounded when she'd offered him tea from her child's tea set, when she was about six.

"I'm serious. There's a lot that could still go wrong. We don't know what happened in Lana's village today, or what the soldiers will do when she goes back. But I think Lana and I will be safer if we split up."

"All right," Darrin said.

Karoline turned to Lana. "Before you go, could you please help me get him upright?"

The two of them worked together, and soon Darrin was standing. With the medical splint making a strong connection from above his knee to below the ankle, he was able to put a little weight on his right leg. Lana departed, heading back for Sunnyside.

Chapter 8

"I'll look for your gun," Karoline said, "but I really don't want you to have to use it."

"Do you think I want to?" Darrin scoffed. "On this crazy planet, the thing is as likely to explode in my hand as it is to actually shoot. But I'll feel better if I have it."

It took Karoline a quarter of an hour to find the weapon. While Darrin checked it, grunted his satisfaction that it was in working order, and holstered it, Karoline went looking for a walking stick that he could use instead of resting all his weight on her.

At last they were ready. Leaning on Karoline's shoulder, Darrin took a tentative step away from the tree, pushing off with his left, undamaged leg. He very slowly began putting weight on his right leg.

Karoline felt him flinch. "Careful! Lean on me as much as you need to."

"It's not that bad. Besides, you're too small to take much of my weight."

Karoline frowned. Why were people always underestimating her? "I am not. I'll be the one to say when it's too much for me. Besides, once you get your balance, you can use the walking stick, too."

Darrin grimaced and leaned on her as he quickly put his weight back onto his left foot. One step.

"Good," Karoline said. The man was heavier than she'd thought, but she wasn't about to tell him that. "That wasn't too bad, was it? We'll just take it as slow and easy as you need, and you'll be back at the camp before you know it."

Darrin paused to look at her. "Don't you patronize me, young woman. If your friend doesn't come back with a wagon or at least with two strong men, this will be a long day for both of us."

Karoline lifted her chin and put her hand on his back to steady him. "Well, then, we'd better get started, right? See if you can use that stick, too."

"You," he said, "are a strong-willed person. All right, let's go."

They'd hobbled much of the way to the road when they began to hear soldiers approaching—two men on horseback, chatting like friends.

"Here are two strong men—just what we were hoping for," Darrin said. "I'll give a shout as soon as they get a little closer."

"No, wait. Let's see who they are first. If they're up to mischief, finding you and me together would be a perfect opportunity for it."

"Then we mustn't let them find us together," Darrin said. "You stay hidden here, and I'll just, uh, hobble out from among these trees and confront them."

"No, you need to get help."

Darrin raised a questioning eyebrow.

"Some of your men are loyal to you, you know." Her voice wavered.

He stiffened. "I would hope they all are."

Karoline bit her lip and said nothing.

"All right," Darrin conceded. "While I'm distracting them with talk, see if you can sneak back around them and go find those soldiers you say are particularly loyal."

"And what if these men kill you in the meantime?"

"You have an overactive imagination. I am their commanding officer. I have no intention of being shot by my own men. And if either of them tries . . . I swear by Death Himself, I will have the man flogged, and if that doesn't kill him, I'll demote him to the ranks and let the soldiers do it."

Karoline shivered. This was not at all how she'd imagined her adventure would turn out—but at least Darrin seemed certain he'd survive a death threat. And he hadn't said he'd shoot the man.

Two men on horseback flashed in and out of view, a trick of Eden's mists, and then they appeared solidly on the road. One was Lieutenant Valdar, and the other, the sergeant who had threatened the child's life yesterday. They rode side by side, talking in a language Karoline didn't know—perhaps that Kestran that Orton had mentioned—and laughing occasionally in a sly way, as if they were enjoying tales told at someone else's expense.

Darrin took three steps forward, leaning heavily on his walking stick. "Lieutenant."

The two men drew up their horses. They stared at the captain, and then looked at each other. "Why, Captain," Valdar said. "When you didn't come back yesterday, we thought—that is, we *feared*—you had been kidnapped or . . . worse . . . by the partisans."

"And you were just heading over to the village up the road to—what? Exact retribution?"

Karoline began walking as quietly as she could away from the conversation, in the direction of the soldiers' camp.

The lieutenant stiffened. "We were hoping that with a few simple threats, they might be persuaded to release you."

"And if they did not?"

The lieutenant shrugged. "As you said . . . perhaps some kind of retribution would be in order."

Now that she'd put a bit of distance between herself and the others, Karoline allowed herself to turn and take one last look at them.

Darrin drew in a deep breath, visible in the movement of his back and shoulders even from this distance. "That will be unnecessary, Lieutenant. As you can see, I am neither kidnapped nor dead. Now, let's go over to the village and straighten things out."

The lieutenant looked Darrin up and down. "You are injured. Perhaps there are partisans still hiding in these woods."

Karoline's heart skipped a beat. She took a step backward, breaking a dry branch that made a loud cracking noise.

The two men on horseback both looked her way.

Karoline turned and fled.

From behind her came a noise that sounded like the cracking of the branch that had betrayed her, but much louder. Something whistled past her ear at great speed. It struck the side of a tree just ahead, digging a channel through the bark and showering splinters.

Darrin's voice: "Stop!"

There was another loud crack behind her. A horse whinnied. Yet another loud crack, then two more.

Then silence.

She ran for another minute . . . two . . . three, then slowed.

And stopped.

If she kept on like this, even she would lose her way. She was breathing hard and could feel her heart pounding, as much from fright as from exertion.

In a few moments, her heart calmed and her breathing returned to normal. She wondered if she should continue to the soldiers' camp. If Darrin had been killed back there, then the lieutenant would be in charge, and her own appearance would seal both his story and her fate. No, she didn't dare go there now.

Karoline turned back toward the place where she'd left Darrin, walking as quietly as she could. Would she find anyone alive there? She wondered whether she could handle the sight of three dead and bloody bodies. But she had to know what had happened, and so she'd have to deal with whatever she found.

If either the lieutenant or his sergeant was still alive, would they be lying in wait for her? This thought set her heart to pounding again. Karoline stopped walking and put a hand to her chest. Did she dare to return? Perhaps the best thing would be simply to go home and leave all this mess with the army behind.

But . . . there was the captain.

What if he had been wounded in the gunfire? What if he lay dying and needed her help?

She had to help him.

Or did she? The man was, after all, a soldier—an enemy of her people. It was one thing to help a man who had sustained a serious injury that was, in a way, her fault; but in this case, the soldiers should be able to take care of their own.

But what if they didn't? What if they didn't get there in time or never found him at all? And there he was, bleeding and hurt, and she could have saved him but was too afraid to try.

No, that was not acceptable. If she was going to act like an adult, she had to consider what kind of adult she wanted to be. It was a person's duty to God and to other people to help someone in need. If she left now, she would be failing in that duty. Karoline refused to be the kind of person who would turn away from responsibility.

Besides, Darrin had made a bargain with Hendrik and with her, and it was a bargain that would keep all the villages between here and home safe, sparing who-knew-how-many lives. The captain must remain alive so that the bargain would be kept.

She took a deep breath and cautiously walked back toward the spot where she'd left Darrin. As she approached, she could hear rustling noises and an occasional grunt of effort. At least *someone* was alive, then, but who? She went carefully from tree to tree, trying her best to remain unseen.

Darrin was dragging himself along the ground toward the road. Two horses stood in the road, shuffling nervously at the smell of blood that hung in the air. She saw a strange bundle of cloth on the back of one of the horses; the saddle of the other was empty. Where were the lieutenant and the sergeant?

"Darrin!" Karoline called the captain, but her voice came out in a whisper.

He must have heard something, for he turned to look in her direction, his expression a mix of puzzlement and pain.

She stepped out from her hiding place. "Are you all right?"

"Never been better," he said drily. "Just a little scratch here"—he touched a finger to his left shoulder—"where a bullet did not slice through my throat."

She came toward him, looking closely at the place he'd indicated. Blood ran down his arm in a steady trickle. She'd seen worse back home, this would heal. "Can you stand up?"

"With help, I think so. I was just going to see what's up with our friends over there." He indicated the road and the horses with a gesture of his chin.

Karoline could now see that the object she'd mistaken for a pile of cloth was actually the sergeant, slumped in his saddle. The lieutenant lay unmoving on the ground.

"I didn't want to shoot them," Darrin said unhappily. "I'd prefer to give them a good flogging and death among soldiers who have no tolerance for betrayal of military discipline."

Karoline shivered.

"But they didn't leave me much choice when they started shooting at you and then me. I just hope they're not dead, so that we can kill them in a way that's more in accordance with established procedure." He grimaced. "Let's go have a look."

Karoline helped Darrin to his feet. She found his walking stick and brought it to him, aware that her muscles ached when she bent to pick it up. "What about your shoulder?"

"It's nothing."

Nothing! None of this was nothing. Karoline was tired of adventure. She'd had all the guns and blood she wanted for a long, long time. She followed Darrin to the road.

Both horses stamped nervously, but they were well trained, and with their reins dropped to the ground, they stood in place. The sergeant stared unblinking, slumped in his saddle. His blood ran down the animal's side and dripped to the ground. Darrin felt for a pulse, and then shook his head. He poked at the lieutenant's body with the end of his walking stick, and the man stirred, groaning. His gun lay near his hand. Using the walking stick, Darrin carefully pushed the weapon away from the stunned man's fingers. "I hope he lives," he said grimly. "I hope the bastard lives."

A rattling noise up the road grew louder. Karoline looked up, and Darrin did likewise. A wagon flickered into view—a wagon driven by Lana's husband, with Lana sitting by his side, coming back for Darrin. Behind the wagon marched a squad of eight soldiers, led by the soldier named Ken.

"Is that the corporal you were talking about?" Darrin asked.

Karoline nodded. "Yes, Ken."

"I know him," Darrin said. "He's been in the army for a while. Good man. He takes care of his own. If I'd realized he was the one you meant, maybe I'd have been a skosh more careful with Lieutenant Valdar." He turned to look at Karoline. "I guess this is good-bye. But before we go, may I ask you something?"

Karoline's heart gave a little lurch. Despite her sudden misgivings, she said, "Okay."

"Friend to friend, nothing changes. I'm just curious. You . . . you aren't actually a member of the resistance, are you?"

She laughed. "Not yet."

He smiled, but his eyes were sad. "Then I'm sorry to say we might meet again, and under less friendly circumstances."

"I'm glad you're turning back now, though. And since we are being honest, now that you know my intentions, I have a question for you, too."

He nodded. "Go ahead, I'll answer as best I can."

Her heart was pounding. All these years that she'd thought of Hendrik as *her* enemy, she'd never seriously considered the possibility that he might be an enemy of her people. But surely, this was her best chance to find out. "As a future member of the resistance, can I . . . that is, should I trust Hendrik?"

He gave a start. "Hend—You know Hendrik?"

She waited without answering.

"Yes, of course," he said, "you must have seen me with him yesterday. I don't actually know him very well, but I'd say yes. I believe he's a man of his word."

Karoline considered. It wasn't exactly an answer to her question, but maybe it was the answer that she needed the most. "Thank you," she said. "Thank you for everything."

Suddenly shy, her face so hot she was sure it must have turned entirely red, Karoline gave in to an urge to hug the man—for about half a second, and then she got control of herself. "I'm going to go home now. I'm sure you'll be fine."

"Until we meet again," Darrin said, and he smiled at her.

Chapter 9

Karoline approached her home with caution. She was tired and hungry, and possibly dirtier than she'd ever been, but all she could think of was her mother and Hendrik. She'd been gone for nine days. Her mother had known that she'd left on purpose, hoping to overtake Hendrik. Probably, for most of those nine days, Marta had thought Karoline had found Hendrik and continued with him. But Hendrik would already have been home for a full day—plenty of time to disabuse Marta of that idea. Now, they would both be worried, or angry, or both. Karoline noticed she was rubbing her hands down her dress, straightening its folds. She made herself stop. She wasn't ready to face them.

Karoline dismounted and led Blaze to the barn. Fortunately, no one was around. She took off the saddle and bridle and put them away. Because she was tired, she groomed the horse as quickly as she could, and then gave him some hay. She promised herself to return for a more thorough grooming after she rested. After she dealt with Hendrik and her mother.

She tried to slip into the house unnoticed. It was mid-afternoon, a bright day full of golden light and flashes of color in the mists. She hoped that her mother might be out working in her garden, or visiting someone. Anywhere else but in the house. Karoline wanted time to wash up and change into clothing that wasn't torn, to make it look as if nothing of any significance had happened to her.

Marta wasn't home, but Karoline wasn't that lucky with Hendrik. As she came in, she saw him, his back to her, writing something at the kitchen table. Her heart sank. She was definitely not ready for this. She swallowed hard and decided to give Blaze the more thorough grooming she'd promised. She turned to go out again, hoping Hendrik might meanwhile leave the house.

But Hendrik must have heard her open the door, for he stood and faced her before she could close it. "Karoline! Where hast thou been?" He was using that no-nonsense now-you're-in-for-it parental voice that he was so good at. "Thou might have left some word, so we wouldn't worry."

Her knees felt weak. After all she'd been through, after the soldiers, the betrayal, the killing, all the dirt and grime of hard travel, now she had Hendrik's anger to deal with. She just wasn't up to it.

"I'm sorry," she said, her voice not much more than a whisper.

"Sorry? Thou *shouldst* be sorry. Thou art rude and poorly raised. Thy mother is worried sick about thee."

Her mother was worried, but not Hendrik. Instead, he was finding fault with how her parents had brought her up. That was just like the man. Worse, he was still thouspeaking her, like a little child. Oh, he could make her so angry! No longer so tired, Karoline balled her hands into fists so hard her knuckles turned white. "And where have *you* been, Hendrik?" Her anger infused her insolence with heat. "I have been to the same places. Do you understand? *The same places.* And now we're both back home again. So, if you'll excuse me, I'd like to wash up a bit."

She moved to pass by him toward the sink, but he took hold of her arm. "Not so fast. What did you mean by that?"

At least he wasn't thouspeaking her. This was an improvement, though still harsh. "I meant that I followed you. I saw you meeting with that captain. I heard you discuss—"

"Quiet." Hendrik looked around from door to window and back again. His eyes were wide, the whites evident. "You did not hear anyone discussing anything, do you understand me?"

For a moment, Karoline wondered if Hendrik might harm her, but no, of course he would not. Whatever else he might be, Hendrik was a devout person. To her own surprise, she realized she had no desire to harm him, either, not by word or by deed. The antipathy between them was petty, a small thing, and she wanted to end it.

But it wasn't that simple. She carefully removed his unresisting hand from her arm. "Perhaps I didn't hear . . . enough to understand everything that happened. But I could tell that you have a relationship—an *ongoing* relationship—with a captain in the Black Lord's army."

His face reddened, and he drew a breath.

Karoline held up a hand to stop him from speaking. She went to the sink, primed the pump, and splashed water over her face. That felt much better. She shook her head and said, "I'm not accusing you of being a traitor. I could see you were trying to prevent the army from advancing any farther toward Meadowcreek, and you seemed to accomplish that."

There was more to Hendrik's journey, of course. What had he said back there? "You have influence over us"? And "enter into communication with you"? Yes, something was definitely going on—something he wasn't going to tell her. And why should he? Neither would she tell Hendrik about her own experiences with Darrin and the soldiers. They both had their secrets. She could live with that.

"Yes, of course," he said. "I was protecting us. At my request, the captain gave his word that the soldiers will not advance farther toward Meadowcreek."

"I know," she said. She also knew that the soldiers would not be advancing at all, but turning back toward Castle Rock, the concession she had gained from Darrin. "And I can see why you don't want me talking about it—in case somebody might take something the wrong way."

He seemed to relax. "Exactly."

She moved past him to her room and found her hairbrush on the table. "Don't worry, I can keep a secret." There were so many knots in her hair. She brushed carefully, to avoid pulling too hard. "But tell me, what do you think is going to happen when the captain and his men go some other way?"

His eyes narrowed. "Meadowcreek will be spared, of course."

"And what about the people who live in the villages that are in the captain's new direction?"

Hendrik looked right, left, right again. "Well, that's up to them, of course."

Karoline put down her brush and folded her arms across her chest. "I disagree. We are leaders of the resistance. Not just the Meadowcreek resistance, but *all* of the resistance. Getting the soldiers to turn back was up to us, too, not just to the unfortunate people in the captain's new path."

"Karoline, I did everything that was possible. I may have saved our lives, so the resistance can continue. You have to learn that there are limits to what one person can do." He stood rigidly straight and put his fists on his hips. A challenge.

She didn't want to get into an outright argument, so she took her time looking for a ribbon to tie her hair back. "So, you agree that it would have been better to get the captain to go back to Castle Rock?"

"In theory. Yes." He stretched out the words in a way that said he was humoring her. "But—"

"And in practice, Hendrik." It was so hard not to let her temper flare.

Disbelief was written all over his face.

"That's right," she said. "Why do you think I took the extra time?"

"Oh, right." Sarcastic laughter added syllables to the words. There was only contempt in his eyes. "Of course. You, the girl-hero of the resistance."

Karoline didn't feel the least bit like laughing. She lifted her chin so that despite the difference in their heights, she was looking down on him. "I am completely serious. The captain's name is Darrin, in case you didn't know."

The blood drained from his face.

Karoline pulled her hair back and tied a bow, tied it good and tight. "He agreed—he *promised*—he'd turn back." She studied Hendrik's face. "Do you think Darrin is a man of his word?"

Hendrik looked away from her steady gaze. "Yes. Of course I do. That's why I went to talk with him in the first place."

"So do I, Hendrik. So when you tell the story of what *we* did when we were *together* in Sunnyside, you can truthfully tell them that the Black Lord's army has turned back. As for the details of any negotiation, as for who exactly was the one to persuade him, well . . .You can claim all the credit. I won't say anything any different, but I want something from you in return. Two things."

He stiffened.

"First, I want you to tell my mother that I was with you. I want you to tell her that I was a great help to you on your trip."

Hendrik made that smug, self-righteous expression she despised. "Lying is a sin, Karoline."

"Yes." She met his eyes without flinching and tried to make her face look sad. "Lying *is* a sin. I suppose I'll have to tell her that I followed you, and then of course she'll be curious, so I'll probably also have to tell her what I saw, and what I did."

He looked around once again, as if expecting Marta to materialize suddenly within the room. Then he lowered his voice. "Even if I told her, she wouldn't believe thou wast with me. I came home yesterday, and I was as surprised as anyone that thou wasn't here."

"Then tell her we were together until the very end, and you thought I'd ridden on ahead while you . . . I don't know, make up something. So of course you were surprised I wasn't here yet, but other than that, I was with you the whole time. And I will say that we got separated and I waited for you, and that's why I was late."

Hendrik averted his gaze and said nothing for a long moment. "Very well," he said slowly. "Since thou hast returned safely, no harm will have been done. I'll speak for thee."

"And that brings me to the other thing. I have traveled on my own for nine days and returned safely. I have acted as an adult, and a partisan, and a member of the resistance, and from now on, I want to be treated like one. I don't want you to thouspeak me anymore."

His lips tightened, but he said, "Very well. But remember, we have an agreement."

"I will refer to you any questions about what *we* did on *our* journey." She paused for effect. "You can tell them we convinced the soldiers to turn back. Not just aside. Back. And it will be the truth, Hendrik, I swear it." She gave him a tight smile.

After a moment, he returned the smile, relief written in his expression. "Two partisans on a mission," he said. "And perhaps indeed you *were* a great help."

She had never realized until that moment quite how much Hendrik's acceptance mattered to her. Her smile spread wider. There would be no soldiers in her story, and no guns. There would be no army camp, no blood, and no betrayal. No captain of the Black Lord's army whom she hoped to see again, someday, when there was no more fighting on Eden. Only her father's grown daughter on her first journey as a member of the resistance, and a stepfather that she might, just might, actually have a relationship with. "And now, please, I'd like to go see my mother. We shouldn't leave her worrying any longer than necessary. Will you go with me?"

Hendrik returned the smile, but his eyes still held questions. Of course they did. So much remained for them to work out. But he nodded and said, "Of course."

<<< >>>

Thanks to Readers

Dear Reader,

Thank you for reading *A Warrior of Eden*. I know that your time is limited, and I'm honored that you chose to spend it with Karoline in her struggle to join the resistance and make a difference for her beloved home world of Eden.

If you enjoyed this book, please consider posting a review on Amazon, Goodreads, Bookbub, or your blog or website. Word of mouth is also welcome, please tell your family, friends, and fellow readers.

If you'd like to see more of Karoline and her fellow Edenians, consider reading *Freeing Eden*, which takes place a few years afterwards and features Kell, a clone of Karoline's father, as well as

Karoline and Darrin. Here, you will meet the Black Lord in person, and discover his dark secret. The series continues with *The Last Lord of Eden* as Kell, Karoline, and Darrin move to the Federation's capital to continue their struggle to keep Eden free.

To be notified of upcoming releases, author interviews, appearances, blog tours, and giveaways, and to receive special content that's for newsletter subscribers only, please sign up for my monthly newsletter at www.gskenney.com. Here too, you can follow my travels, still only on planet Earth.

To follow me on Facebook:

https://www.facebook.com/gskenneyauthor

To follow me on Instagram:

https://www.instagram.com/gskenneyauthor

Again, thanks so much for reading!

G. S. Kenney

p.s. See the next page for an excerpt from *Freeing Eden*...

FREEING EDEN

By G. S. Kenney

Set back a few feet from the street by a tiny but well maintained garden, the entry to the autobrothel looked inviting. The sun had nearly reached the tops of the buildings on the street's west side, and the garden lay in shadow, its cool, green humidity freshening the air around. The quiet street, with its well maintained and tastefully ornamented buildings, was a pleasant respite from the market, where merchants hungry for a sale accosted passers-by in the streets to hawk their wares, and where by late afternoon the air was heavy with the odors of sweat, leather, cooking oil, pastries, perfumes, and garbage.

No sign announced the name, although the traditional cast-from-brass emblem, a stylized pair of wings, hung beside the heavy wooden doorway. A matching brass knocker was set in the center of the door. Zara reached for the knocker. Its metal was cool under her fingers.

Then she hesitated.

Did she really want to do this?

After a long, hot day dealing with dishonest merchants in the market, she had decided to quit early and unwind. She could still head back to the ship. A quiet drink alone in the ready room, maybe a little music, and—

No, that didn't sound appealing at all. Zara spent half her life alone aboard the *Winged Princess*. She didn't mind the solitude, but when she was planetside, she wanted someone to talk to. She wished she knew someone besides old Elleren here on Lesurat. The old man was one of the near-homeless who hung around the spaceport hoping for a few coins in return for a kind word. He'd taken one look at Zara, fresh from a month alone in space, and recommended this autobrothel. She'd smiled and thanked him and given him all the coins in her pocket, almost a tiyu, never imagining she'd actually end up here.

The knocker had grown warm under Zara's touch.

She wanted to talk, and given the choices, a baseclone in this place might serve nicely. She'd transported an entire shipment of baseclones a couple of standard years ago, from Bigollo, where they were made, to the mining complex on New Mars. That hadn't been a bad run, not bad at all. She'd reconfigured the cargo area for habitation by the dozen or so baseclone units and given the supervisor a berth in the passenger quarters. Once the ship rotated into the tiny dimensions, bypassing normal lightspeed limitations, the trip to New Mars out on the edge of the inhabited part of the galaxy had taken six weeks. Zara had had time on her hands and helped the supervisor care for the baseclones.

They had no intellect, those failed clones. No language; no human curiosity or initiative. With their remote-control units shut down, the devices attached to the back of their necks at the base of the skull, they were as warm and receptive as sleeping puppies. They would sleep endlessly if they were not awakened and exercised. She'd fallen into mothering even the big, bearded ones twice her size. They'd been easy to talk to, totally uncomprehending of course, not even awake, but in their way gentle and sweet.

Yes, perhaps this autobrothel would be just the thing. She'd find some poor baseclone and talk to him for an hour or two. Of course he'd listen and never once interrupt or argue or try to persuade her to buy something. She'd give him all the motherly affection she could. It would be a pleasure for her, and—who knows—perhaps in some deep recess of his being, the baseclone would be glad of it, too. Zara smiled in anticipation and knocked on the door.

A moment later, the door opened. A middle-aged man with dark, curly hair and nondescript features, shorter than she was, assessed her. "Yes?"

"I . . . uh, I wanted to . . . rent a unit." Knowing what the man must be thinking, Zara felt the heat of a blush on her face and was grateful that her dark skin hid it.

"Spacer, eh?" When the man smiled, he looked younger, and kind. "Well, don't just stand there. Come on in." He opened the door wider, stepping back to allow Zara to pass. The room beyond was wood-paneled and carpeted with richly designed rugs of an Ancient-Earthish pattern, geometric designs in warm reds, pinks, blues, and tan. Vases of sweet-scented flowers and bowls of real fruit graced tables that stood near softly inviting couches and chairs that picked up the colors of the rugs.

Zara nodded her appreciation and stepped inside.

"Please. Have a seat." The man motioned toward one of the couches, and sat nearby as Zara sank into the soft cushions. "There's no need to be shy, you know. Lots of people come here. Spacers especially. All the time." He paused and smiled at her. "What kind of unit would you be interested in? We have all kinds, all price ranges, from robounits to baseclones."

"Oh. I didn't realize . . . I'm looking for a baseclone. Something *human*."

The manager coughed discreetly into his hand. "I must advise you that neither robounits nor baseclones are considered human, legally speaking. But I do understand. Many people prefer the more human feel of the clones. But the establishment does not allow certain activities with the clones that may be done with the robounits. Baseclones are expensive, and we don't want to see any harm come to them."

Zara's face grew hot again. What kind of pervert did he think she was? She drew herself more upright. "I'm not interested in *activities*," she said stiffly. "I just want someone to talk to for a while."

For a moment, the manager fumbled for words. Then he said, "We welcome your business, of course, and perhaps it isn't in my best interest to say this. But surely you could find a less, ah, expensive alternative for talking. A shop, perhaps, or a bar. Any merchant . . ."

This was the last thing Zara wanted to hear. "I have been talking with merchants all afternoon. I'm tired of people trying to sell me cheap goods at high prices. That's exactly what I'm trying to get away from."

"Forgive me." He looked as repentant as a sinner at the altar. "I ask these questions so that I can match you with the best possible unit."

"Oh." Zara brushed back a loose strand of her thick, curly hair, and tucked it into her hair band. "Well, go on, then."

"Do you prefer a male or a female?"

"I don't know that it matters." She thought of the baseclones she had transported to New Mars. They had all been male, all gentle. "Male, I guess."

"Ah, good, good. And, to confirm, you're certain that it's only talking you want . . . or listening, to be precise? The unit will neither talk nor understand you. You do know that?" He held up both hands, palms out, a gesture of pacification. "I just want to be sure."

"I've been around baseclones before. I know. I can do enough talking for any two people all by myself."

He smiled. "I happen to have a unit available now that is, if I say so myself, one of the very finest on all Lesurat. A real treasure." He shook his head appreciatively and clicked his tongue. "But I wasn't planning to put him into service for another week or two. We just acquired him. He's new out of the tanks and not yet conditioned for physical intimacy. The restriction will be in your contract." He gave her a meaningful look.

"Yes. That's fine."

"I think you'll be very pleased with this unit. If, of course, it's in your price range."

Zara hesitated. "How much?"

"I can rent him to you for five hundred tiyus, half of what we would charge in a busier time."

The amount was a month's salary for a skilled worker on Lesurat. Zara scowled. "It had better be a good unit."

"In all my years in this line of work," the manager said, "and of all the baseclones I've dealt with, this one is the very best." He looked at her slant-eyed, then quickly added, "For talking, I mean. Obviously, we don't know yet about his other . . . uses."

✳

The baseclone sat calmly on the couch in the private room, looking straight ahead. But as the manager opened the door to let Zara in, the unit turned his head toward the sound, tilting it slightly in a gesture that resembled curiosity. He watched her with an utterly naive openness, and waited.

Zara smiled, and perhaps he might have smiled too. Or she might have imagined it.

"Hello," she said nervously after she closed the door and locked it. Zara had enjoyed talking to the baseclones she had transported, and though they were completely passive, she had been able to imagine that they enjoyed it too. Like small babies, they brought out a maternal side in her. And besides, after all the time she spent alone, she needed to unwind. She hoped this clone would act the same way as the others—just patiently appear to listen. "It's okay," she explained to him, laughing a little, "I talk to myself, too."

Zara broke eye contact with the unit and looked around the room. It contained no bed, perhaps to discourage "activities" such as those forbidden in Zara's contract. The color scheme ran from cream to gold to the rich russet of the soft carpeting, suggesting refinement and wealth. Next to the couch where the baseclone sat was a table flanked by two chairs. The table was made of a smooth, blond wood, solid wood, not a laminate. She knew how much she could get for it, and the price took her breath away. This autobrothel must cater to a very discriminating clientele indeed.

On the table stood a bowl of fruit, a crystal carafe of water glistening with condensation, two goblets, a bottle of red wine, and two wineglasses. It seemed unlikely that the unit would be able to drink from a glass by himself. Perhaps the second glass was simply for show. Zara couldn't help but wonder in what state a few hours of "activities"—to use the manager's word—would leave such a room, and marvel at a quick calculation of the establishment's maintenance budget. But the tranquility of the room appealed to her, and she nodded slightly in approval.

The baseclone watched her but didn't move. Zara walked over to the couch. "I'm Zara."

He looked at her with what might have passed for interest, moving slightly to make room for her as she sat beside him. The manager had been right; this was a particularly fine unit, far more alert and responsive than the mining units. Unlike them, he seemed almost human. Almost a trueclone. He was also—Zara nibbled at her lip as she studied him—there was no denying it—beautiful. His dark blond hair framed a face that could have been aristocratic, with long, elegant eyebrows and eyes that were to die for. They were a bright, noontime-sky blue, ringed in midnight blue. Zara tried to imagine this clone's creator. She had no way of knowing, of course, but she pictured a handsome man of late middle age, graying at the temples. Perhaps he was the head of a great business empire, or of one of the clandestine crime families, or perhaps a prince. He would be, Zara decided, a man of depth and contradictions, not some squirrelly little back-room accountant, but a man people would follow. It was a good fantasy—but the baseclone hadn't been long out of the tank. His cheeks were still covered in an almost translucent down, the beard not yet starting to grow in.

"You are an unexpected pleasure." Zara found herself reaching toward his cheek. "Uh-oh. Maybe that's outside of my contract." She pulled the contract up on her comm as he watched. "No . . . it says *intimate physical activity*. I'd call this friendly, not intimate, wouldn't you?" She reached out again. "Is this all right?"

She lowered the tone of her voice slightly, answered for him, "Yes, of course. Your wish is my desire." She stroked his arm lightly, enjoying the blond hairs on it and the dry warmth of his skin. "You are quite lovely, do you know that?"

With his other hand, the baseclone reached out and stroked Zara's cheek. She drew in a breath of surprise. None of the mining clones had ever initiated action, not unless their remote control units were turned on, and even then, of course, only if someone signaled through the control unit. She felt at the base of his skull and found the dataport. No remote control unit had been inserted. *One of the very finest units on Lesurat*, the manager had said. *A real treasure.* Zara had to agree. She'd had no idea baseclones could be so responsive on their own.

She closed her eyes and relaxed. A few more moments like this and the manager would be breaking open the door, angrily flourishing the contract. Zara sighed. She took the baseclone's hand and held it so that it wouldn't wander toward places that suddenly and unexpectedly ached for his touch. "Tell you what. We'll take turns. I'll tell you something about me, and then you tell me something about you. Or I'll do it on your behalf. Your records seem to be appended to this contract." Not that his records contained anything of interest: baseclone registration number; date of disposal on Bigollo; date of arrival on Lesurat; duty tax paid.

At seventeen thirty local time, a low, melodious chime sounded in the room.

Zara sighed. "Thirty minute warning."

The clone had his arm over her shoulder, and she rested her cheek contentedly on his chest. She could feel his heart beating, and his light breathing stirred her hair.

"I hope you've gotten used to all my talking by now." She twisted beneath his arm so that she could face him. "Wouldn't it be wonderful if you could talk, too?" Zara stroked the clone's cheek, and a slight smile came and went across his lips. "I almost believe you could." She looked longingly at him. "And then I would say, *Hello, my name is Zara. Za-ra.*" She pronounced the word carefully. "And you would say, *My name is*—Now, what would your name be?"

"Kell," said the baseclone.

Zara pulled back, her pulse pounding. "What? What did you say?"

The baseclone looked at her with his habitual open gaze, head slightly tilted, as if waiting for something that didn't really matter. He said nothing.

Zara felt a lump in her throat, coupled with an almost desperate urgency. "Please. Please say it again. What is your name?" He watched her silently, and then hesitantly touched her cheek—for all the world as if he were trying to comfort her.

Zara took his hand away from her cheek, kissed his palm softly, and then wrapped the hand firmly in her own. She met his gaze and held it. "Tell me your name. Please. I really want to know."

A tear rolled down the baseclone's cheek, and then another, and Zara felt that her heart would break. "Why are you crying?" she whispered. "Have I hurt you? I didn't mean to." Softly, her fingers traced the track of the tear down his cheek.

Watching her as if mesmerized, the baseclone spoke, slowly. "My . . . name . . ." There was a pause long enough to make Zara believe that he would not speak again. Then he added, ". . . is . . . Kell."

Zara let out the breath she hadn't realized she was holding, and she allowed herself to fall back against Kell's chest. He wrapped his arms around her.

"Kell," she repeated.

The chime sounded two long tones.

Zara sighed. "Twenty minute warning. I can't leave you here. In this place. This life. By all of space, Kell, you are *not* a baseclone. There's no control unit in your dataport, but you've been watching and responding to me. I could begin to believe there might be some kind of advanced baseclone I don't know about who can maybe do some of that, but you—! You have feelings—you were crying. And you understand me and can answer; that means you have some intelligence, and you have language. You're not a baseclone, and you don't belong here."

She stood up and walked to the mirror that was mounted on the wall opposite the couch. Straightening her hair's disarray, Zara watched him in the mirror, watching her.

"The papers attached to my contract show you were discharged as a baseclone, but I can't believe it." She took out her comm. "I've transported baseclones, so I have access to the discharge database on Bigollo." She spoke the access code and her password and authenticated her identity with a thumbscan. "I'll use your ID number from the contract." As data appeared on the small screen, she frowned, shook her head, and rekeyed the number.

She shook her head again, more stubbornly. "Something's wrong here. The database on Bigollo says that you died in the tank, and the body was disposed of a month and a half ago." She rubbed the goosebumps on her arms. "But clearly you're not dead, because a couple of weeks ago you turned up here on Lesurat, a baseclone with no name and no owner. But that's false, too. You're a trueclone, not a baseclone. So what's going on?"

He watched her openly, patiently.

"I can't get into the database of creators. There was no need, since I was dealing only with baseclones. There's no clue in the data I have as to who or where your creator might be."

The chime sounded several times, insistently.

"Ten minutes. Not enough time to figure this out. So let's just focus on the urgent question, which is, what are we going to do about it?"

She began pacing up and down the small room. "If the administrators on Bigollo knew you were a trueclone, you wouldn't have been sold here. So most likely, they don't know. That means all I have to do is tell the manager, and he will do the right thing, whatever that is. Return you to the lab, I guess, so that your creator can be found and notified."

She sighed again and turned back to Kell. "On the other hand, this is Lesurat we're talking about. That man is as greedy as the rest of them. Even if he's honest, he'll want very much to doubt me. His purchase papers are in order, and so are the baseclone discharge papers from Bigollo. He'll rely on them. He'll ask himself, *What would a spacer know?* and he'll answer, *Nothing. She's mistaken.*"

Zara pulled at Kell's arm. "Sit up straight, Kell. I'm talking to you. We have to figure this out, and we don't have much time."

Kell obeyed.

"If he's not so ethical, the situation will be the same, or worse. He'll pretend very graciously to accept my comments and thank me profusely and just continue doing what he's doing with you." A shiver ran down her back. "I can't bear to think about that."

As if sensing her distress, Kell touched her arm gently.

"Thanks, Kell." Zara managed a smile that she hoped would pass for reassuring. "You are so much more than a normal baseclone. But touching is not what I need right now. What I need is an idea. I don't suppose you would have that?" She looked at him quizzically, not entirely sure that he wouldn't, but Kell said nothing. He watched her impassively, waiting.

Zara sighed. "No, I suppose not. If you'd had an idea, you would have been out of here days ago, right? I guess I have to figure this out by myself. So, let's see . . . we aren't going to get any help from the manager here. That means it's up to me. Kell, listen. If I can get you out of here, would you want to come with me?"

Zara studied the clone, but his open expression didn't change, gave no clue to what he might be thinking. *If anything*, she reminded herself. But he looked so vulnerable that her heart ached. "Now, come on. Answer me. If I'm going to put myself on the line for you, I need to know how you feel about it. Would you want to come with me?"

Those beautiful blue-in-blue eyes studied her, seemed to be giving the question some thought. But he didn't answer.

What had she expected?

"Yes."

Zara jumped. "What?"

"Yes," he said. "With you."

Read more of *Freeing Eden* at
https//www.amazon.com/product/B07RCYSBCV.

Acknowledgments

John Donne famously said that no man is an island. This is especially true when it comes to writing and publishing a book. It's time to acknowledge the other people who contributed to this book.

My parents instilled in me a love of learning and taught me the values of respect and community that I hope infuse this book. My husband Daniel Kenney, above all others in my life now, has supported my writing career even when, sometimes, it meant sacrificing his own time with me. Sweetie, I hope this book makes it feel worthwhile. My children, now grown, were my first beta readers way back when and encouraged me to publish my stories long before I felt ready. I see a lot of Karoline's character in the adults you have turned out to be, and don't worry, I mean that in a good way.

James Frenkel, my agent and meticulous editor, has also become a good friend, constantly encouraging me. And Debby Gilbert of Soul Mate Publishing, awesome publisher of the other two books in the *Ascent of Eden* series, has been so supportive in my effort to self-publish this one. Thanks, too, to Julie of JS Designs Cover Art, who created this wonderful cover, and to Laurie Cooper of Pub-Craft, my marketing guru and mentor, and now also a friend.

One of the best things that ever happened to my writing career was becoming a finalist in the 2018 Golden Heart contest of the Romance Writers of America. A lot has happened to the Golden Heart and to RWA in the interim, but my cohort of Golden Heart finalists, the Persisters, are some of the most generous and supportive people I've ever known anywhere—as well as an incredibly talented group of writers.

Other writers are crucial to any writer for support and feedback. I'm fortunate to belong to two critique groups. Not only have these conscientious readers helped make my books better, but they've also kept me writing to a schedule when sometimes it was the hardest thing in the world to do. And Jeanne Estridge, a fellow Persister, writing partner, and friend, helps me remember to show up at the computer, even when I can do no more than staring at the screen.

And you, gentle reader, thank you for opening your heart and mind to these books. I hope to see you again in this journey.

With warmth and gratitude,

G. S. Kenney

www.ingramcontent.com/pod-product-compliance
Lightning Source LLC
Chambersburg PA
CBHW070411200726
48294CB00003B/1161